CLONES
FROM
THE FUTURE

Case Wong

Copyright © 2021 Case Wong

All rights reserved. No part of this publication may be reproduced, distributed, or transmitted in any form or by any means, including photocopying, recording, or other electronic or mechanical methods, without the prior written permission of the publisher, except in the case of brief quotations embodied in critical reviews and certain other noncommercial uses permitted by copyright law. For permission requests, write to the publisher, addressed "Attention: Book Rights and Permission," at the address below.

Published in the United States of America

ISBN 978-1-955243-44-5 (SC)
ISBN 978-1-955243-45-2 (Ebook)

Case Wong
222 West 6th Street
Suite 400, San Pedro, CA, 90731
www.stellarliterary.com

Order Information and Rights Permission:

Quantity sales. Special discounts might be available on quantity purchases by corporations, associations, and others. For details, contact the publisher at the address above.

For Book Rights Adaptation and other Rights Permission. Call us at toll-free 1-888-945-8513 or send us an email at admin@stellarliterary.com.

Contents

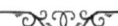

THE FIRST FIELD TEST 5

THE TIME-TRAVEL DEVICES 10

TESTING DESTINY 12

MUTUAL ATTRACTION 15

CONSEQUENTIAL FATALITIES 23

SURPRISE, IT'S DEATH 29

GOOD FRIDAY 33

HER MISSION 38

THE WATERWAYS GARBAGE-CLEANUP TEAM 44

LIONS AND LAMBS 50

SEEING INFINITY IN MIRRORS 54

LETHAL WEB WEAVERS 56

BACK TO THE PRESENT 65

BENEFIT OF THE DOUBT 73

A SKEWED TIMELINE 79

THE DARK TRIAD 85

THE SPLIT PERSONALITY 93

PSYCHO THE SCORPION	100
THE ABLE SELF	109
VELLIAN THE SPIDER	114
MACHIAVELLIAN	120
IMAGINATION	124
NARC THE SNAKE	127
THE FOURTH OF JULY IN 2021	133
EASTER SUNDAY	150
PROPELLING DREAMS	155
THE UNFORESEEABLE	165
PRESCRIPTIONS	175
THREE AGAINST ONE	192
DARK TRIAD'S MASCOT	200
SPARKLER SPARKS	205
THE DEADLINE	216
THE LOOP	219
EPILOGUE	224

THE FIRST FIELD TEST

*B*aby boomers were born between 1945 and 1964. Professor Harry Chinn—who liked feeling accomplished and proud when he compared his generation to the younger generations—was sixty-five in the early spring of 2018.

The moon was bright above a quiet gas station where a downtown streetlamp shone on a parked police cruiser. The baby boomer's time-machine eyewear fit snugly above the false moustache and beard he had on.

Harry strutted by the gas pumps in his disguise, the driver hopped out when he walked right up to the car, and the two men stood face to face.

"May I tell you your future," Harry asked.

"What the...?"!

The uniform and badge did not hide his true colors—he could see right through him. In *his* eyes, the thuggish officer was just another common criminal, at heart.

"I want you to know what will happen before it happens."

Trying not to lose patience, the lawman breathed deeply.

"Do you want to get shot? Take one more step and I'll oblige you," he said with one hand on his holstered gun. "Your message better be worth my while, you old fart."

"I'm wearing time-machine glasses. I've foreseen this moment and the inevitable moments to proceed, twice. I foresaw how our encounter would've played out earlier today. I say 'would've' rather than *will* because I played this all out two times. What I foresaw *last* is what will happen. No, I'm not a nut who's getting cute with you." He touched the dial by his left temple. "I'm watching a few seconds ahead of time in order to live like an echo at the moment."

"I'll tell you what's about to happen. I'm bringing you in off the street, you babbling menace."

"Please wait. Truth be told; you would've taken me down right now." Harry *sigh*ed. "Getting in your backseat is my choice. Yes, you *are* taking me in and then I'll explain myself to your superiors."

The cop, while failing miserably at staying calm, saw him step up to the backseat door and reach for the car-door handle.

"Hey," he yelled at Harry.

The policeman stepped in close enough to stop him and he tried to grab his wrist, but Harry spun around with surprising speed—in one fluid movement, the professor chest-bumped the man, reached out, and took the gun from its holster.

"Get down on your knees!" While staring down the barrel of his own gun, the lawman did as he had been commanded. "It worked, *yes!* By the way, I went over this moment *three* times, not two. I foresaw what just happened and then *let* it happen. Yep, what's foreseen *last* is fate, as long as the foreseer lets destiny be." Dr. Chinn felt like rejoicing. "You suck. You don't discern enough, your judgment sucks! You ought to be more discerning."

While keeping the gun's aim locked on the officer, he opened the car door with his other hand and hopped in the driver's seat. Stepping out from the gas station's washroom was the cop's partner.

"Yes, I am serious! Hand it over," she heard Harry yell.

The oversized washroom key tag dropped to the pavement. The tires *screech*ed. The cruiser kicked up a dust cloud for both cops to choke on as Mr. Chinn sped away.

"Come back here with my damn wallet!"

"He took your wallet?"

The cruiser pulled into a shopping mall parking lot. The inventor parked, hopped out, and with a spring in his step, he approached the sportiest car parked nearby. Its wing-like car door spread open with the touch of the door handle.

Harry slid into his cherished high-performance vehicle and, grinning widely, he chucked the man's wallet out the window while thinking to himself, *serves him right*. As Harry reflected on his reasons for disliking him, he stopped grinning. *Let's hope that no-good excuse for a lawman didn't recognize me.*

Turning the key sparked the ignition. Putting the pedal to the metal, he tore off into the night.

Harry stepped inside a cottage. In the washroom, he unglued his press-on facial hair. He prepared a cheese plate in the kitchen afterwards.

He took the cheese into the master bedroom. Despite that designation, this was not a room meant for sleeping in—seeing as how it had been converted into a lab. The bed was replaced with his "pin-pricking tool", and he plugged the fortune-telling eyewear into one of its jutting sockets.

He called it "the Beyond". He felt it calling for him in the recent years. Compelling him!

The pin-pricking tool was up-and-running by the end of last year—it's an inter-dimensional porthole. He tapped into the Beyond with it.

This machine *seemed* as big as a grand piano, but it was even bigger on the inside! Its four-dimensional structure surpassed the third dimension—the tool twisted inwardly and outwardly upon itself like a tesseract.

Tinkering with highly-modified tech at his lab table, he was back on the job—the *second* time-travel device would soon be ready.

THE TIME-TRAVEL DEVICES

*T*he snug-fit eyewear had two main knobs. Its left knob was the fast-forward shuttle. This dial would enable you to witness future events through the eye lenses and built-in earbuds. Yes, you'd gain foresight with these glasses on.

Its right knob controlled time travel in the physical sense. You'd use that dial to bring your future self into the present.

You could, for example, reach out a minute ahead and reel in your "older" self. Your "clone" from the future would then *pop* in on you. You then would vanish sixty seconds later, only to immediately reappear in the past and meet *your* one-minute-younger self. But, when the one-minute mark comes around once more, it would be your younger self who disappears from the present to reappear in the past moment that happened sixty seconds ago—while you keep on being yourself.

We can time travel from the future to the present. We *cannot* travel from the "true" present to the past. Consider it. Suppose you went back in time and somehow killed your younger self. If you died in the past, however, then you couldn't have come from the future to begin with.

"Nobody can travel back in time AFTER one's own death—that would be paradoxical," the professor told Miss Soffy. "The laws of time travel prevent the paradoxes."

TESTING DESTINY

*H*azel Soffy was about to turn forty. She embodied a plain-Jane style.

With a Polaroid camera in hand and while wearing Harry's time-travel device, she stood facing a white wall. At her feet were two full paint pails and paint rollers in an empty tray.

Her fingers tweaked the right knob. The eyewear hummed, tickled her face, glowed to a cool white, and a pulse of force shoved Ms. Soffy a few stumbling steps backward—all the while her eyewear remained put, suspending in midair! The light grew from behind the lenses of the time-machine glasses.

In that light, matter materialized out of thin air. First,

the eyeballs formed. Next, the face took shape, followed by the head and hairstyle. The naked body was forming from the neck down in the bright-white glow too. The light sucked back inwards with a *pop!*

A swirling breeze cut through the room's still air and a fully-formed naked woman now stood with her back to Miss Soffy—'twas her clone from the future. She handed her time-machine glasses-wearing, nude, future self a nightgown.

"What time is it," asked the older one.

"Seven-o-one."

"It was seven-ten when I felt the transport coming on. You start becoming me in roughly nine minutes."

"What color did you paint it?"

"Red."

"Then now, we'll make it blue."

They each picked up an unused paint roller. They poured *blue* paint into the tray. The identical twins soaked their rollers in blue.

They finished painting in minutes. She shot what they had done with the Polaroid camera. This photo proved the wall to be blue. The one from the future told her to "paint it red" when she relives this moment.

"Yes, I'll paint it red," the younger one replied while reading her watch. "It's seven-ten" were her last words before vanishing into thin air.

In that same instant, what they painted blue changed to the color *red*. The paint rollers and tray were suddenly covered in red paint too, even though, in the last ten minutes the wall was, without a doubt, painted *blue*!

The one wearing the nightgown was left all alone.

"Now, the most present version of myself is *me*."

Miss Soffy examined the snapshot taken a minute ago. This photo—which *was* of the blue wall—NOW showed the red wall. These past ten minutes happened in time for nobody else except Hazel Soffy and her clone from the future.

MUTUAL ATTRACTION

*P*rofessor Chinn was renowned in the scientific community for his inventions. His main income source came from the patents he held. NASA acquired lots of his stuff.

Harry also globetrotted around to speak at schools. His topics used to vary, but since last year, "time travel" had become his sole focus.

"Chance" encounters seem to happen in the world. One might wonder if magnetism has something to do with it. Do imperceptible spiritual magnets—compelling forces that can override our conscious choices—attract us to each other, sometimes?

The Soffy's lived in a farming town, a two-hour drive

from the city. Hazel was a middle child growing up in a household of seven. That number dwindled as her siblings found their places in far-away cities and as grandpa died in the front yard while taking the garbage out. The bed-and-breakfast was then left for her parents and Grandma Emily to run.

Hazel came back to the family farm in the winter of 2018. She was single, turning forty, and not too thrilled to be either. Miss Soffy tried her best to live the big-city life for the past six years. She blamed those years.

"I should've had a better time," she told herself. "It didn't feel like Grandfather Time was watching over me while I struggled in the city. Where WAS the great one when I needed him?"

She also wanted to stop seeing herself as being a failure. *I failed to "fit in" with the city crowd*, she often thought. That feeling of failing was upsetting her, even now, as she walked inside the Soffy's Bed and Breakfast.

That's alright, though. The countryside made her feel capable of coming to terms with her presumed failure.

Her sense of self was intact when she left the farm. There was a time when she would agree with her family and friends that "Hazel Soffy deserved to be trusted and cherished." She *was* a "somebody".

She referred to the rat race as being "deadly". The will to compete could be *felt* in the rat race. Her neighbors' desires to get ahead, by stomping on others, were like fangs digging into her throat.

Although her neck felt those imaginary bites every time she stepped out, there's still hope. She'd always leave her apartment thinking, *I can grow to trust and cherish this city, even if it is deadly.*

On the streets and in the shops, she competed for attention against mobile devices. Today's generation freaked her out daily. Everybody answered to digital screens rather than everyone else. Her name for today's society was "the Pixilated Generation".

In Hazel's opinion, getting attention had everything to do with spending money these days. The only times Hazel seemed to feel any "love" from strangers were when she was opening her purse.

"Rather than money TRANSACTIONS, we'll rely more on human INTERACTIONS, someday," she would hope aloud.

Common sense was breaking down. The world's digital screens had everybody focusing on the two-dimensional. Life, however, has more than two dimensions.

Exploration was an activity now confined to those flatly

depthless screens of ours—dividing us all apart from the real world and from each other. As for her "sense of self", the city did not seem to care who she was.

What everybody apparently cherished and trusted was also in 2-D. What they wanted was flat and lacking depth: cash. A sense of self didn't matter. What mattered was money.

The people around her appeared to be stashing it away. They liked to hide their money from everybody else in the world as if, rather than SHARE a thing of beauty publicly, it's better to keep that special something a dirty secret. Yeah, right, as if.

Miss Soffy would not turn a blind eye. She saw how badly the rich want to hide their wealth and in her head, she cried, *a dark and dirty personal closet is no place for any glorious treasure! Come on people now, reveal the treasures.* Alas, what once was the means to an end now became the goal but, in Hazel's head, *wanting money only for the sake of possessing cash makes no sense.* In this world, where the end goal was money itself, people were not valuing the virtue of generosity like they should. *To hell with coveting money!* Eventually, the deadly rat race stripped her of what little savings and borrowings she had. *Oh well, at least my heart still grows thicker.*

If it was not for her faith in angels and their ability to thicken one's heart, she could've lost all hope in the big city rather than be back at the farm right now.

Morning sunshine bounced throughout the restaurant. Hazel's parents were glad about not having to man the bed-and-breakfast today—they were grateful for the free time being given to them by their daughter.

Miss Soffy busied herself with shining utensils. There wasn't another soul in the joint until Harry strolled in.

Even Harry did not know why he chose to rent a cottage in her sleepy township. He selected it randomly on a map. Nobody in town knew him and his time machine was not even operational, yet. He must've been brought here by intuition.

"Can I have your big-breakfast special, please?"

Hazel and Harry talked about the weather first. The conversation seemed effortless, flowing from one topic to the next—they both wished to quit being loners, you see. His reason for being here came up—he told her about the time machine.

"So, you specialize in time travel? Fantastic!"

Was she humoring him? He could not tell.

"What if I told you my time machine won't be a fantasy?"

"Then, that'd be a shame. I *love* fantasy." She was being serious. "We need fantasies. Anything fantastic always reminds me of how the truth will always be true, even if we can't prove it for a fact."

Hazel did not believe unicorns, fairies, and mermaids to be *real*. What she considered "real" was that MAGIC which comes along with fantasizing.

This magic she was referring to "is real enough to make us feel like BELIEVING." She explained how fantasies make room for our growth: "We can all unite and grow through fantasies. They're like buffer-zones. A fantasy acts like a bubble around me. I grow inside it. The bigger the fantasy is, the larger the bubble gets, and the more room I have for growth. Other people's fantasies also help me grow. The fantasy of reeling yourself in from the predestined future is actually making me fantasize about having the ability to control time and now, it feels like I'm growing."

She made an argument for equality too: "If we were to compare our fantasies, mine ought to be considered as equally fantastic as yours. Making us equals in a way."

She picked up his dirty dishes and served him a dessert.

"We are equals. I agree, fantasies are practical to have."

Time travel, however, would soon be a matter of fact.

His pin-pricking tool was running on auto back at the cottage as they spoke, hardware configuring and programming the eyewear.

Their conversation tickled him pink. What was it about her? Was she extraordinarily special? Even though they were technically "strangers", he still felt sure about one thing: the world is better off with her in it.

Harry imagined a "Cloven Tongue Like as of Fire" hovering over her head. The Book of Books mentioned such a thing. He could picture the floating fiery-orange tongue which split at the end like the toes of a hoof.

It's written how, after Jesus ascended to heaven, His disciples spoke at a mass called "the Jewish Feast of Pentecost". There had arrived, in the thousands, Jewish pilgrims from all over the Roman Empire and beyond.

Now, there *was* a language barrier between all those in attendance. For Jesus' disciples, that language difficulty disappeared when they were filled with the Holy Ghost.

According to Luke: "Suddenly, there came a sound from heaven as of a rushing mighty wind, and it filled all the house where (the disciples) were sitting. And there appeared cloven tongues like as of fire, and it sat upon each of them."

The disciples then went outside into the milling crowds

who were from different nations. The disciples then "began to speak with other tongues as the Spirit gave them utterance". As the word got around, the amount of people who came to listen grew and "every man heard them speak in his own language".

Even though Harry knew she was speaking English, in his head he pretended that her lips spoke an *alien* language while the Cloven Tongue Like as of Fire obliged him with the translation. Harry never imagined a fiery cloven tongue upon anybody else before, so he took it as a sign.

He had the urge to make her a proposal right then and there. Harry asked himself, *what do I propose?* For him to suggest any kind of sexual intercourse at this time would've been inappropriate to say the least. *What can I propose?*

"You're offering me a job in the time-travel business? What?" She couldn't believe her ears.

CONSEQUENTIAL FATALITIES

Today was Dr. Chinn's 90th birthday. His hair was whiter than ever. Dawn's light basked Harry's face as he awoke on his deathbed. The old man sat up to face a grandfather clock.

"I'm up right on time," he said to himself. "I've got three minutes."

Those few minutes were spent trying to remember what his subconscious was dreaming of right before awakening—the one last dream he'd ever have. The minutes were up—with a *pop*, the old man disappeared. All that remained of him were the pajamas he had on.

This old man reappeared near his cabin in the woods wearing nothing except for his time-travel glasses.

"Put this on," he heard a voice say.

The nude old man turned around to face his sixty-five-year-old self who wore a jacket with the number "two" painted on the back and he was referred to as "Number Two". He handed his naked elder self a bathrobe.

Another Harry stepped out from behind a tree. He was also sixty-five years old but, younger than "# 2" by twenty-four hours.

The original one and his two clones from the future stood face to face. By their feet were several grenades duct-taped to a baseball cap.

"I remember *dreaming* right before y'all brought me back here," said the ninety-year-old.

2 replied, "I know what you're going to say. I'm from tomorrow. I heard all about your dreams yesterday. In your dreams were luminescent little fishes. They swam up from the deep and bit into a super-massive chunk of fish food floating on the surface."

"Only the moments I've been through can be remembered. I haven't lived passed anytime beyond right now. I have foreseen this conversation we're having, though," said the original one.

The ninety-year-old said, "I foresaw *and* remember living out this exact moment."

"This morning, the glasses showed how you'll blow yourself to kingdom come pretty soon," the youngest one said to # 2. "The eldest among us will immediately be erased from existence when you die. I'd be left here all alone. I'd live to be ninety. Now, I'm proposing we alter the foreseen future. Let's decide to change our minds." The original Harry put on the grenade hat. "Let's kill *me* instead of Number Two."

"Bad idea," the oldest one objected. "You're the original one. You're the one who brought us here. We are your clones. You were here first. You are the youngest."

2 nodded *yes* and added, "I can't come from the future if I'm presently dead."

"I disagree," he said to his elders. "I think it doesn't matter which Harry Chinn dies. What matters is having at least *one* of us alive in the present. So long as we *all* don't die, Harry Chinn will remain among the living!" He said to the eldest: "you live to be your age because *I* kept on living. But, if I die today, who is to say Number Two won't live to be ninety? How come *he* gets to die? Why can't it be me?"

"We don't even have to actually go through with the killing. We've already foreseen the results," said the ninety-year-old.

2 stared hypnotically at the grenades and said "no. We're going through with it, period. It's not real until it *is* real." There was a sparkle in # 2's eyes. "This conversation freaks me out. Yesterday morning, I foresaw what we are now talking about. Later in the afternoon, I re-enacted this exact discussion. Right now, I am re-enacting yesterday's re-enactment. This moment is 're-enact-mental'! Or better yet, let's call it a 'RE-ENACTUALIZATION'."

"Don't be foolish. It'd be impossible for me to be here now if I died at the age of sixty-five."

"I've glory in my guts. Let me prove my courage," the youngest pleaded with grenade hat in-hand.

"It's too bad the time machine only works on people, or else we'd have tested this on animals," said the eldest.

2 snatched the grenade hat from his clutches and put it on as the other two walked away to take cover behind a nearby boulder where two police riot helmets sat.

2 stood alone in the small clearing and felt the grenades against his skull—how cold, hard, and smooth they were. He cautiously touched one grenade's pin and carefully slipped his index finger through its ring. The other two stuck out their shielded heads from behind the boulder.

"Yeah, keep your heads up so I can see y'all. I want to see myself as being ALIVE," # 2 roared as he pulled out the pin and laughed heartily. *KA-BOOOM!*

He took off his riot helmet. Blood and fleshy bits stained its visor. The explosion had scattered bloody body parts everywhere. The eldest Harry was gone too—nowhere in sight. The original one was now by his lonesome in the woods. His hand picked up the time machine.

For no particular reason, Harry started thinking about last night—he was remembering the cop. How shocked he looked while staring down the barrel of his own gun. *The man had it coming to him.* How fun it was to take his wallet and car. *That is what you get for being an inconsiderate bully.*

His mind delved further back to sometime last month when he witnessed a few petite Asian women in handcuffs being shoved out the door of a low-rent massage parlour by that very same cop.

Harry happened to be strolling along the corridor at the time—to visit a friend in the office building—and was passing by the police arrest taking place. That cop held a clear-plastic bag containing all the money the ladies had, and in his other hand was a half-full plastic water bottle.

Not only did he confiscate their earnings, but they will also probably get jail time and fines—those poor little women, he thought while witnessing one lady ball her eyes out as the policeman smirked smugly at them, and as his smug smirk was making Harry's insides rage and wallow, the cop's partner stepped into the corridor holding an empty plastic water bottle. The cop noticed his partner's eyes scanning the hallway.

"What are you looking for, Peterson?"

"A recycling bin," she replied.

Harry was even more appalled by what he did next: that no-good excuse for a lawman took the plastic bottle from her and then tossed both bottles in a regular trash can—a bin meant for non-recyclable garbage only! This encounter, by the massage parlour, was the first time Harry laid eyes on him.

The second time the inventor saw the cop was yesterday morning when he FORESAW him at the gas station—last night, Harry fulfilled that premonition. The question on Harry's mind now was: *would we have once again crossed paths, at the gas station, if I did not possess the precognitive device?*

When owning a pair of Chinn's glasses, one might wonder, *am I the one deciding my fate, or is it ultimately decided by the eyewear?*

SURPRISE, IT'S DEATH

𝒦nowing everything there's to know about your own death sucks! It'd be on your mind constantly. *Is my death timely or untimely? How can I prevent it? Do I even want to prevent it? How do I live to the fullest?*

It's probably better to not know. If fate was ever knowable, then changing the way in which your fate gets sealed would mean that you do not trust destiny.

What would then become of your FAITH in destiny for heaven's sake? No, faith ought to always be required.

With Chinn's time machine, you could foresee your own ultimate demise. It would be pointless, however, to fast-forward past the moment you die. After that point, the eyewear always showed nothing but continuous static—like an antennae signal gone dead on TV.

Harry had no desire to witness his own death. The moment before the snow of dead air was just too precious for him to watch.

With the time-travel device, you're able to divert the course of time. To alter destiny, or not, was a matter of choice.

Chinn knew he'd meet his maker at the age of ninety. He was able to alter the future, though. He could skew the timeline by making a choice. Rather than pass away on his ninetieth birthday, there was a fifty-fifty chance he would choose to die tomorrow instead.

It was Thursday. Yesterday, he exploded his own head with a grenade hat. Today, he sat with Hazel on the cottage's deck to bask in warm sunshine. They both wore time machines.

"Do you actually enjoy being obsessed with the future," she asked him. "Don't you find the present to be more meaningful than the future?"

"On the contrary, I am being present. Right now, I'm here being interested in the future. Are you not having fun? Is the future not interesting?"

"Interested? You bet I am. Although, I'm finding it hard to find any interesting future times. How do you pinpoint which moments are worth foreseeing while in super-fast forward?"

"The need-to-know stuff jumps out at me whenever I'm in 'the zone'. You watch life fly by with your eyes and ears too much. Forget about the sights and the sounds. Let your heart and guts tell you when to re-hit the play button. Relax," he said. "You'll be one with Zen soon enough."

The stars filled the sky above the rented cabin. The 4-D object had been hooked up to the computer which was running a complex diagnostic test onscreen.

The professor typed keyboard commands with amazing speed. His forehead crinkled at the data flashing before his squinted eyes.

Harry's "mirror self" from the Beyond—the identical version of himself in a parallel reality—suddenly appeared on the monitor. Upon seeing himself on the screen, his eyes widened and a smile grew—*eureka*—the system's glitch appeared to be fixed.

From within the monitor, his mirror self could see into the lab. His onscreen eyes watched himself run a cable from the computer to the time-travel device he wore.

He turned his back on his onscreen mirror self, keyed in a code, held his breath, and pressed 'enter'. The eyewear vibrated and tickled his face as it glowed coolly.

Cool whiteness shone brightly, from behind the lenses, onto his face. This was it—the moment of truth.

What followed next was a *swoosh, pop, zap, zing,* and a *pow!* From then on, the glasses only showed the hissing, fuzzy, snowy static.

He then took the device off and the afternoon sun blinded his naked eyes. She was still sitting beside him on the patio. He turned to her.

"Hazel, I will *die* trying to go back in time tomorrow night."

GOOD FRIDAY

He felt like time was drawing nearer by the second. 11:11 pm was a mere hour away and if he did not dare make his attempt when it arrived, then this one chance at going back in time would be forever lost.

Yesterday, the professor foresaw himself failing to correctly calibrate the pin-pricking tool in time for it. The glasses, mind you, became active only a few weeks ago. If only he had more time. Harry feverishly tinkered with the 4-D machine with Hazel at his side.

"A phenomenal cosmic energy will come from the Beyond to channel into the tesseract in less than an hour," he told her. "I have a solid theory about the coming of this glorified power but, not to sound too technical, let's just say: at eleven-eleven tonight, the eyewear will send me backwards to arrive at any point in the PAST I choose."

"But the laws of time travel will not let us go back from the present to the past due to the paradoxes. YOU taught me that."

"I don't care about paradoxes anymore."

"You're crazy. Yesterday, you foresaw how tonight's experiment will kill you."

"I'll die only if the pin-pricking tool is set on my *previous* settings. Those calibrations don't matter anymore, I'm now making the RIGHT adjustments to the machines. It'll work this time around, for sure!"

"But you've already re-calibrated the machines twice and had just foreseen the outcome of your test once more." She rhetorically asked, "and what, pray tell, did the eyewear reveal the second time around?"

"According to my *second* premonition of tonight"—he became embarrassed— "I'll choose to abort. I fail to go through with it."

"Right, you'll come to your senses before it's too late. You realize how foolish it is to risk your life in the name of science."

"Hazel, our SOLE chance at literally 'making history'

comes in less than an hour from now."

"No, you know there's more than one chance. There are TWO chances. The precognitive glasses revealed one more coming on Easter Sunday."

"True, but the power coming from the Beyond on the morning after tomorrow scares me. It's *too* powerful." A spinal chill made him shudder. "I've done right by devoting myself to tonight's more manageable cosmic blast." He checked his watch and gasped.

She shook her head. "Please make me a promise. Say you'll foresee once more BEFORE you attempt to harness the Good Friday energy in the tesseract. Only go through with it if you foresee its success. Promise?"

"I do."

The door shut behind her as she left. Using the other pair of time-machine glasses, Hazel flash-forwarded to tomorrow morning when she'll apparently be having cheese for breakfast on the cabin's patio with Harry. This Saturday, being shown to her, was the same as the last one the inventor had watched.

First, you use the glasses to see the future. Secondly, you choose whether to alter the future or not.

Harry stopped re-tweaking the pin-pricking tool at

10:50 pm. The variables he had overlooked were now accounted for and everything seemed to be in order.

The power would channel into the 4-D tool in about twenty minutes and nothing more needed being done except to use the eyewear once again. He did so and foresaw himself...

With a time machine on his face, he rechecked the cable connection between the tesseract and the computer. The clock read 11:10 pm when he typed in the last line of code. At 11:11 pm, his finger hovered over the enter key…and hovered…and hovered. The seconds passed and yet, his finger still hovered over that key. It became 11:12 pm. Meanwhile, his trembling finger remained suspended above the enter key.

Harry took off his foreseeing glasses with a *sigh*. "WHY will I always chicken out," he cried out loud. It was now 10:55 pm—sixteen minutes to go. "Wait a minute, hold on. Could *knowing* my future be the problem?"

Taking into consideration destiny's course, Harry considered the time when he watched himself die. He then realized what his problem was.

"Yes, of course! Having witnessed my own death, I'm now too afraid to take the test tonight. Knowing the future is what is making me gutless!"

It's his destiny to NOT have the courage when the time would come fifteen minutes from now. KNOWING his original fate was what took away his courage.

He then decided on doing what must be done in order to alter his fate. He chose to throw caution to the wind and NOT rely on the flash-forwarding ability.

Ten minutes until the phenomenon arrives. One final command was keyed into the computer—a spontaneous last-minute readjustment. Harry then broke his promise to Hazel by deciding against foreknowing what happens next.

The eyewear was hooked up to the computer and back on his face by 11:09 pm. The moment of truth was now truly upon him this time. When the time was up, he held his breath.

HER MISSION

*D*o you believe there's more to life than the "physical world"? A great number of people do. They say we're all unaware of the "spiritual plane" hidden in the world.

The material plane, being the densest of the planes, lies beneath the spiritual. "Denseness" allows for matter and energy to be visible. The five senses detect the physical world because it's so dense.

One can be driven wild by the sensual realm of the material world. There's always just so gosh darn many pleasures in life which we each love looking at, listening to, feeling, smelling, and tasting—such as the things money can buy.

Money, ever since after its invention, had become an element of much worry for the material world. From forests being converted into condos to the consumer garbage dumped into our water supplies and the pollution we breathe in—money keeps impacting on Earth's landscapes.

It also might've kept people out of touch with the spiritual plane. Due to money's power over the material world, the physical plane might repulse the spiritual one—be it either the repulsion of the little angel on your shoulder, or of Karma, or of any other divine intervention for that matter.

To illustrate, take for example the thieves and con men who thrived in the big city. Did they not end up buying more security for themselves with their stolen and dishonestly obtained money?

Not only did they have expensive, beefed-up security to shut out the ones they robbed and swindled but, the selfish ways of those money grubbers also scared spirituality away.

By the end of Hazel's six-year stay in the city, she was clinging on for dear life to the spiritual plane's edge while a demonic monster jumped up to take swipes at her dangling feet. At least, that was the metaphoric embodiment of a nightmare she sometimes saw projected on her own eyelids.

It looked like a six-foot tall hairless man with crimson skin, deadly-sharp teeth, ten finger claws, and no genitalia.

Its tongue could extend six yards and slash flesh like a lashing whip—a useful weapon for ensnaring prey with. Hazel had visions of the monstrous tongue lassoing and squeezing people in order to quickly drain them of their will: to fight back, to move, and to even breathe.

Her nightmarish demon-man sprouted from underneath the material world and surfaced onto the physical plane to hunt down anybody who acted as a spiritual beacon.

Hazel Soffy had a grip on the spiritual plane and the man-demon wanted to tear her away. It wanted to consume that which the spiritual found attractive about her, and she was terrified.

An even freakier thing about it all was: although Hazel was capable of foreseeing, there was still no way she could have foreseen tomorrow's fight against that hellish freak. In other words, Miss Soffy had no idea she would be battling her demon tomorrow morning—in-the-flesh.

It was the day before Easter Sunday. Hazel wore pajamas to breakfast. She set a cheese ensemble on the patio table while basking in the morning's glory. The sun felt as soothing as the crispy fresh air. It felt like the weather was radiating love.

While wishing she could be one with the glory, Hazel

nibbled on cheese. Harry devoted two shelves in his fridge exclusively to cheese. What was with his obsession with the dairy anyway?

Perhaps the inventor was at his best when he was feeling cheesy. Miss Soffy felt differently; her case was not the same. Push too much cheese on her and she'd throw up.

Wait. She read her watch. He was destined to be with her right now, so, where's Harry? *Something is wrong. Oh no.* She scooted back inside thinking, *there is only one other place he could be.* She hoped to find out that she thought wrong.

She swung the door open to see the pin-pricking tool fluxing in four dimensions as usual. Harry was lying face up on the floor and motionless with his legs sticking out from behind the tesseract. His sprawled-out body had a sudden, twitchy spasm as she approached.

When a flaring electric bolt streamed down the cord running from the computer to Harry's eyewear, he had another spasm and as her hand took the time machine off his face, she felt an electric sting, *zap!* Upon seeing him without the glasses, her stomach churned and she felt like throwing up.

It was as if his eyeballs were scooped out with an ice-cream scooper. Another electric bolt shocked his body again. She felt cheated by the false hope being given by his bodily movements. You would not need a medical school diploma to figure out that Harry Chinn was DEAD.

"Did you not see this coming," she cried and fell to her knees. "What the…? Did you use the glasses, yet went ahead with killing yourself regardless?" She sobbed. "If only I was here to stop the suicide." She shook her head *no. Harry killed himself. NO WAY. How could this have happened? Did he break his promise to me and NOT foresee this?*

She wanted answers. Hazel's attention drifted from the corpse—her eyes were being magnetized by a handwritten note on the desk. Beside the note was a computer memory stick atop a thick stack of files. The note read:

Dear Hazel,

If you're reading this, then I am dead and my death will be nobody's fault but my own. I am sorry but, my only chance of success comes from breaking my promise to you. I cannot foresee this night again. You see, every future we foresee stems from us firstly using the glasses. Unfortunately for me, I will *always* foreknow myself as being too gutless to test my theory tonight. So, now that I have made the final re-calibrations, in order to change my destiny of failure, I must refuse the temptation to *know*. I must go on faith alone.

The files on the coffee table contained many pages. Some notes were typed. Others were handwritten. There were complex mathematical formulas, schematics, charts, and diagrams. The data did not make much sense to Hazel—it was all over her head.

What could be done about him being gone? She felt powerless. How could she *not* feel powerless? It was not like she could turn back time or anything.

Or...could she?

"Hold on," she told herself. "I do have a chance at altering history." She remembered herself saying last night, "there's more than one chance. There are TWO chances. The precognitive glasses revealed one more coming on Easter Sunday."

Pushing herself, she walked away from his body. The tesseract magnetized her attention. Its space-age design—which was a mind-blowing image to behold—squeezed through her pupils and touched the mind's deeper recesses. Another phenomenon was coming *tomorrow*.

She wanted to save his life. A powerful blast from the Beyond would channel through the pin-pricking tool on Easter Sunday. Yesterday was Good Friday. She was on a mission. Her goal was to traverse history and prevent his suicidal mistake—the deadline: 8 AM tomorrow.

THE WATERWAYS GARBAGE-CLEANUP TEAM

he sharper you look, the smarter you feel, she thought while changing into business-meeting attire.

Miss Soffy had decided on reeling in a clone for the mission considering how the best assistant would be none other than herself at the top of her game in life.

Hazel utilized the glasses to shuttle ahead through time. Soft and loud images flashed forward before her eyes. Hours went by in mere seconds.

She caught a glimpse of later today when she'll be arguing with her future self in the lab. At a speed five times faster than normal, they both sounded like chipmunks.

The outlook sped up. Nighttime zoomed by, daytime melded into the day after tomorrow, and Easter Sunday became yesterday.

Hazel slowed down for a closer look. Harry apparently will not be around at any time *after* Easter Sunday. She set the glasses on 'pause'.

She was obviously unsuccessful in bringing him back—not a problem, though. Change can happen since she now knew *that* future.

Success remained possible in *this* future. Failing in the future did not matter. It was about what happens in the present.

The world sped up again. Time flew by too fast to fathom life's situations. She took Zen into consideration. She felt in her heart and guts like pressing the play button right about…now.

A year had passed and not much has changed in Hazel's outward appearance. She was sitting on a bench surrounded by grandiose buildings and spectacular billboards on a humid day in a South Asian city. The concrete setting stretched outward to seemingly no end.

The pedestrians everywhere were Oriental mostly and there were hardly any automobiles around. She noticed an iPad, on this Hazel's lap, displaying a mathematical formula in Harry's handwriting and with a finger-swipe came a hand-drawn diagram of his pin-pricking tool on the next digital page.

The time machine then zipped one day ahead to reveal her one-year-older self on a beach in the Philippines and facing over a dozen predominantly female locals holding up a chest-high banner which read: THE WATERWAYS GARBAGE-CLEANUP NON-PROFIT ORG.

By Hazel's side was Tara Candido—a co-worker who was directing the commercial that's about to be filmed. Tara was behind the camera and facing her fellow Asian colleagues standing behind the banner.

"Show the camera the feeling of fulfillment you get from being an environmentalist," Tara shouted. "Let's show everybody the love we have for our boss: Miss Soffy!"

Hazel walked closely behind Tara who was filming The Waterways Garbage Cleanup Team excitedly competing for face time with the camera's lens like teenage girls in the front row of a live rock-and-roll performance on the Ed Sullivan Show.

Meanwhile, as Miss Soffy watched her future staff's commercial shoot, she realized with a smile, *I will earn a living as an environmentalist in a year's time.*

Right now—back at the cottage—the images of sitting in the Orient while finger swiping through the data on the iPad was the premonition being taken into consideration. Telling by how confused she looked with iPad in hand, it became clear that one year just would not be enough for her to learn the ins and outs of it all.

Don't reel in this one, she decided. *She needs more time to understand his inventions.* A more knowledgeable clone from the future was required—one who had confidence in the mission's accomplishment. Time, however, was slipping away fast in the meantime. *I'm taking too long looking for the ideal me.*

She slumped onto the sofa and let her eyes wander. She stared at the ceiling fan, the fireplace, the doors to other rooms, the staircase, the open kitchen, the chairs, the tables, the carpet, the wood flooring, the home-entertainment system, the bookshelves with books, the cabinets, the quaint household ornaments scattered around the den, and out the windows—until her darting glances settled upon the calendar on a wall. That was when the idea came to her like a lightning strike.

With the time machine back on her face, the original Hazel set the destination point to when she will be exactly ten years older: March 31st, 2028.

"If I plan it, it'll come true," she thought aloud. "I *will* be ready and able when I'm fifty because that is the plan." The time-machine glasses sifted full-throttle through the years. "I'll take one last look."

The future flashed before her eyes until it all came to a halt and time settled into normality. On March 31st, 2028, mid-afternoon rain clouds parted and sunlight warmed Hazel's face as she stood alone on a stage overlooking a few dozen onlookers gathered around her in a public square. She used a microphone for the crowd.

"Ten years ago, I ALMOST travelled back in time. Since then, I've been wondering *why* I didn't succeed in traversing history. Today, I'm hoping my past self and me will succeed this time around." She smiled at her audience. "What...don't you think the past can be changed? Or do you think it's too late for me?" She shook her head. "It's never too late." She held up the eyewear for all to see. "I remember using *this* time machine a decade ago. I used it to arrive at this very moment we are sharing. In fact, my younger version of ten years past is watching us right now as I speak, and she is about to send me back in time. Any moment now, I will disappear right before your very eyes. Y'all won't know it but, I'll be reappearing inside a cabin by a lake in the year 2018."

"Can I ask you something," shouted a man in the audience.

"You just did. Next question please." She giggled. "I'm kidding. Come on up here so we can all hear you."

The man was handed the microphone when he hopped onto the stage.

"Time travel is fiction," he told them all. "With that being said, I'm still willing to play along with you. I am a psychiatrist. I might be able to help you with your delusions." He grinned. "Your next destination is in the year 2018, you say? In other words, a decade ago! You will be as old as you are now but having missed out on our last decade. My question is: how do you feel about having to do it all over again at *your* age?"

"I knew you were going to ask me that." She giggled again. "Yes, I want to experience it all over again. Although, I suppose everything won't feel brand new to me like it did the first time." She looked upwardly. "If only I didn't have to remember. Doing it the second time around must be better without the memories."

Hazel popped out of existence right before their very eyes. The clothes she wore lay in her place on the stage. Everybody was surprised.

LIONS AND LAMBS

Pop! A swirling breeze swished loose paper around the lab and blew Hazel's hair back. The fifty-year-old Hazel had popped in wearing nothing but the time machine.

She put on leggings and a shirt. From here on in, she was referred to as "Number One".

"It's about cherishing the pinhole" was the first thing "#1" said.

They sat across from each other. #1 took a moment to meditate, inhaling deeply through her nose. #1 then explained how "the goal is to make the pinhole last longer".

In pitch blackness, there's a single solitary spec of white light. It looked like a distant star in deep space. However, it's *not* a star. It's a "pinhole" and its surrounding darkness was *not* outer space.

The only thing keeping the pinhole open was the pinpricking tool. Without it, the pinhole would close shut and be gone.

The Beyond could not be accessed without the pinhole and time travel would then be impossible. The pinhole was the connection. The only way to see it was by crawling inside the four-dimensional construct.

The tesseract's underside had a hatch. Pull yourself up through the hatch and you would be inside a tubular shaft. This tube could fit up to three Hazels if they all squatted or knelt in a tight huddle.

The tube's low ceiling had a round opening—that hole could comfortably fit the upper bodies of only *two* Hazels. Pop your head through it and you would see the inside of a dome.

The radius, from the hole's edge to the dome's circumference, was Hazel's arm-length—when standing erect inside the shaft, every part of the dome's wall was within her palm's reach.

Beyond the dome looked like a cloudless midday sky. The dome's inch-thick wall transparently encased hundreds of soft nuggets. These "nuggets" came in two types:

the "lion's mane type", and the "lamb's wool" nugget.

Each lion's mane type was almost a cubic inch in size, and they all had bronzy-golden fur. Take only the mane from a lion, then shrink it down to form a nugget—that would give you a "lion's mane type", which was twice as big as the fleecy and white "lamb's wool nugget".

The population ratio between the two types was 1:1. Hundreds of these furry and fluffy nuggets drifted all around the bluish dome.

Keeping the pin-pricking tool running was their purpose—every one of them amounted to being the tool's power supply. These nuggets constantly trembled, they became vibrant while trembling, and their combined vibrancy kept the pinhole open.

Lamb's wool nuggets tended to band together. They did so in order to maximize their potentials.

A lone lamb's wool type ultimately produced less fuel than a lion's mane nugget would. A lamb's wool duo, mind you, had the power of *two* lion's mane nuggets.

If you took, for instance, many individuals from the lamb's wool type and matched them with an equal number of lion's mane nuggets, and then isolated the sheep-like ones from each other, the lionesque could overpower them all by a lot. If those sheep's wool nuggets *united*, however, they could *equal* the lion's mane type not only just in number, but *power* too.

On the other hand, the lion-like nuggets need not cluster into groups in order to reach full potential. No, they chose the loner path instead.

At the top of the dome was another hole and it opened up to the pitch blackness. Stare into this opening hard enough and you'd see, way up there, *the* pinhole.

The original Hazel crawled out from underneath the pin-pricking tool.

"I can't believe how much there is going on inside," said the younger one.

"Did you see the pinhole?"

"Yes." Her glances darted around the ceiling. "Where *is* the pinhole located anyway?"

"According to his data, it is in the dimension *between* dimensions."

"So, what now?"

"Cherish the pinhole! It must stay open. Our mission is to keep it from shutting."

#1 then went on to recap her memories of the next several hours.

SEEING INFINITY IN MIRRORS

*T*he Hazel at age fifty, aka #1, remembered what happened ten years ago like it was yesterday. She was the original one at the time.

#1 was also, at that time, on this mission with *her* clone from the future. *That* clone had spoken about decade-old memories of when *she* was the younger one, alongside *her* future self, in the lab.

By sending your future self to the present, you could create a "time loop". Memories from the future might *appear* to be infinitely repeating.

#1 *remembered* her future-self talking about when her ten-years-older clone spoke of *her* decade older version who had the same conversation with *her* clone from the future—and so on and so on it went. It's like when you stand in-between mirrors and see a *seemingly* infinite number of your reflections in both.

So, how many times did Hazel travel from the year 2028 back to the present? "Only once" would be the most logical answer—seeing as how this time loop existed only in #1's *mind*.

The time loop had to do with "*remembering* the future". She was recalling events which have yet to unfold.

Every one of her clones from the future, in this time loop, recalled memories which never happened in "reality". That's because the future can't be a reality, yet.

The future always has yet to exist. Which meant, the only time the Hazel from the year 2028 *pop*ped in on the Easter Weekend of 2018—for real—must be right now on this Saturday.

LETHAL WEB WEAVERS

#1 remembered what's about to happen in the morning. She recalled them both failing at their attempt to harness the Beyond's glorious power and how the mission to save his life was not accomplished. That happened ten years ago—when #1 was the original one.

#1 had spent ten years studying his data, the pin-pricking tool, and the time-travel devices since 2018. For the past decade, Hazel learned everything she could about the cosmic phenomenon's second coming inside the 4-D construct on the Easter Sunday morning of 2018. She had arrived from the future to teach her younger self ways they might possibly alter the fate of their mission.

Now, #1 must not play out this replay in the same way

it was played a decade ago. They must do things differently and better, this time around, in order to possibly stop Harry from making yesterday's suicidal mistake.

It was Saturday afternoon. As the glasses on #1's face powered down, she remembered what *her* "Number One" said at this precise moment in time.

"We're destined for failure! This mission wasn't accomplished when I attempted it a decade ago. Now, this time around, I've foreseen us both failing once again," said the Hazel of ten years past.

That was then. This was *now*.

Twas Saturday afternoon. She turned and faced her original self while wearing the time machine.

"Our fate is to fail! *I* failed this mission when I attempted it ten years ago and the glasses just showed us both failing tomorrow—once again!"

How can a change in the cycle arise? What could they do, this time around, which would alter destiny's course? Try harder maybe? Who knows?

"There's no time to waste," said #1. "Let me teach you how we'll harness the upcoming cosmic blast. You must learn your role before it arrives. Learn fast, for we will be needing time to sleep. We must feel well rested in the morning."

"How do we get an outcome different from the one *you* had when you were my age?"

"I don't know, damn it."

"After ten years of racking your brain, you *must* be fully prepared for this by *now*. You need to be ready. The mission's success depends on your leadership."

"Fast-forward to 7:40 am tomorrow. Watch...and learn."

At 8:02 am on Sunday, they both crawled out from under the 4-D tool in tears and coughing badly. They felt a burning pain in the lungs and their stinging eyes looked puffy. These physical wounds resulted from a "foreign inhalant."

"We're going to be poisoned tomorrow?"

"Yes," #1 replied. "The foreign inhalant is toxic. It comes from creepy web weavers. Harry didn't know about their existence but, I do. During Good Friday's cosmic channelling, Harry's computer recorded the 'deaths' of many fleecy and furry nuggets in the tesseract. Before yesterday, his computer also revealed a strange 'webbing' covering the dome inside the 4-D machine. Harry never knew it but, deadly web weavers had spun those webs and they were to blame for the deaths of the lion types and the wool nuggets in the tool! These killers are invisible. The computer doesn't detect them. Our naked eyes cannot see them. However, they can be seen with time-machine glasses on. They look like prickly maggots. They each prefer to live in hiding. When the lethal web spinners come for both types of nuggets, they'll firstly isolate the prey from one another by trapping them in their webs. Harry's notes speculated that the killer is the webbing. He then programmed the computer to keep the heavenly little hairballs untangled and free, inside the pin-pricking tool, when yesterday's glorious power surged through. He succeeded too—his computer program removed the webs from the dome on Good Friday." #1 heavyheartedly *sigh*ed. "Harry didn't know how futile his efforts were. The killers came nonetheless and poisoned all those lions and lambs in there."

"But...if there's no mention of the creepy invaders in Harry's notes, then, how could you know they exist?"

"*My* 'Number One' let me know about them, ten years ago, when I was *you*."

"Let me get this straight. Right now, you are letting me know about the web weavers, just like how your future-self informed *you* a decade ago. Just like how your future-self got that information from *her* older clone? So... this discovery was passed on and on and on until, finally, it has come to my knowledge. But HOW was it discovered in the first place? And at what point in time was it when our discovery actually got made?" Their eyes squinted and foreheads crinkled.

"What's going on here is, *somehow*, your clones from the future are relaying facts to us which we couldn't have learned on our own and for ourselves at any time."

"It is seven-forty. The attack starts in five minutes," #1 said on Sunday morning.

"The foreign inhalants are still scaring me. Is there *nothing* we can use to breathe better with?"

"No filters can help us. We are dealing with teleporting particles. The foreign inhalant doesn't need to be *breathed* in. The particles will go into our lungs, and form directly on our eyeballs, even while our eyes and mouths are closed."

"What doesn't kill us makes us stronger." The younger one balled up her fists.

#1 crawled under the pin-pricking tool, the original one followed her lead, and the hatch closed shut underneath their feet. They both stood erect inside the tubular shaft and their upper bodies went through the hole above them.

The dome's sky-blue interior made it feel like the outdoors on a sunny day. They marvelled at the hundreds of fleecy and furry nuggets dancing everywhere in the dome's transparent wall.

The attackers started showing up at 7:42 pm and not only did the eyewear make the invisible web weavers visible, but it also magnified them.

"They look like fat maggots covered in spiky tarantula hair. *Gross!*"

"I told you so."

The tarantula-like blobs were each about half as big as a sheep's wool nugget. They numbered in the hundreds and were everywhere, creepily crawling all around the dome. In less than three minutes, the lamb-like and the lionesque would be savagely pounced on.

The web crawlers were a problem in the pin-pricking tool's hardware—no computer program could expel them. Their physical existence was mysterious—the web weavers remained intangible and like ghosts to every material substance except for one: human skin.

"We'll knock all of them off the nuggets like *this!*" #1 gave the dome wall a hard slap with her bare hand. "Brace yourself. You'll feel pain each time."

"I'm not good at getting used to pain."

#1 nodded in agreement. "The pinhole must remain

open. It'll stay open only if there are *enough* lambs and lions left alive when the power surge starts. We've studied their attack pattern thoroughly. Do you remember the moves we rehearsed?"

"I do."

The lab's computer recorded the Easter Sunday onslaught. The attack started at a quarter-to-eight and lasted until 8 am.

#1 memorized, to the best of her ability, where and when each nugget died that day. After committing patterns to memory and upon returning to the year 2018, she redrew the map which would be their pre-emptive defense.

"We must do better than our best. We must try harder than our hardest," #1 said with another heavyhearted *sigh*. "It's overwhelming, I know."

"I'm positive we'll succeed this time around."

As they stood in the dome with their time machines on, a lion type caught #1's gaze. The nugget was like a majestic hairball—pure lion's mane.

Three sheep's wool nuggets spiralled in close above it. Their fleece made them soft on the eyes. They all had finesse. As the group drifted by the loner, all four nuggets fluxed like how living hearts might be able to flux.

#1's palm pressed on where a cluster of golden and whitish nuggets had gathered in the dome's wall and when the first strike came, her hand felt a stinging pain. The glasses uncloaked and magnified the many invaders to show how the maggot-sized enemy streamed up their forearms like marching ants while they frantically swiped them off.

The duo used both hands to slap and backhand the dome, standing back-to-back as they swatted away at the inner wall—the women shrieked in pain every so often.

Each sting released the foreign inhalant. Their eyes watered and when #1 coughed most violently, a speck of blood exited her mouth!

All they had to defend the nuggets with was pre-emptive knowledge and sheer willpower as the attackers relentlessly invading in waves—killing nuggets here, there, and everywhere. The casualty rate grew as the deadline drew closer.

Trying to keep up with the enemy wore down the women. They had been drowning in agony and stress since the onslaught began.

The timer on the glasses showed them having three minutes left. The attack rate grew faster and more widespread as the seconds counted down.

The women tried to keep their defenses up while the will to defend kept on diminishing. Never mind the mental duress and physical pains, the poison had diminished their will!

It felt like being bombarded by insane hatred. She felt anchored, unloved, and naked in a treacherous surrounding. ½ a minute left.

#1 cried out, "Oh God!"

"What do I do next? Help me remember."

#1 collapsed as she fainted. 15 seconds to go.

BACK TO THE PRESENT

She sat across from her original self who took off the glasses, *sigh*ed with despair written all over her face, and was thankful to be already sitting down.

"We'll get creamed in the morning, correct?"

The younger one asked, "Is the pain to come too much for us?"

"I'm not going to lie. Why would anybody lie to themselves, right? We will get hurt, bad. Those web weavers leave scars. You will not be the same after tomorrow. Along with their poison stings comes a voice as mean as evil yelling at you in your head, 'Depart from here and never consider coming back.' The enemy is like a pusher, selling us a one-way ticket to the grave the way they do. Honestly, I am dying to give up and pack it in right now. Let's face it, if we throw in the towel, you'd be saving yourself ten years of headache worrying about, studying, and planning for this mission."

"Yes, but—"

"But…" #1 rhetorically asked.

"There's a flip side to your suggestion. Let's say we do quit now. Then we will also be living with regret for at least ten years. I will be kicking myself for being given the chance to save his life and not taking my best shot at it. Let's not forget who the mission is for."

"What if *we* want him alive even more than he might've wanted to live?"

The original one shook her head. "The inventor didn't intend on dying, his death was untimely. His work here wasn't finished, he wanted to do more. He would've wished to live. We must at least *try!* No guts, no glory."

"You're right."

"Could the enemy have some kind of weakness you might've overlooked?"

"What could I possibly *now* realize that hadn't occurred to me in the last ten years?"

"My elder, tell me how to be of service."

#1 nodded and told her to "go get the map".

She rushed off and hurried back carrying the map #1 had drawn on a large sheet of paper. Resembling the complex football plays coaches tend to scribble on chalkboards, it mapped out where and when the poisonous web weavers kill each innocent and remembered victim inside the tool's dome.

Going over the attack patterns for hours, with barely any breaks, took them into the evening.

The original Hazel sprang off her chair at 7 pm and cried, "I can't retain any more info. If I go over your map one more time, my brain might explode."

"Hold yourself together. Breathe in the air deeply." They watched each other breathe. "Suck it up. Blow it out."

They both stretched out their cramping limbs.

"It's a hectic fifteen-minute attack sequence. How are we expected to take every fatality into account?"

"Study hard if you don't want to fail," #1 responded.

"Why? Will studying harder make me better at serving YOU inside the tool?"

"Yes, you serve yourself through your studies."

"When you say 'you', do you mean me? Or do you mean

yourself?"

"I mean us. We're serving each other for the sake of the future."

"The way I see it, I must serve *you* for *your* sake."

"My future is yours too."

"Fine, tell me what to do and hurry, my elder."

"Déjà vu!"

The sun shone in and on the pin-pricking tool. #1 stopped pacing around to stand silently like a petrified deer.

#1 then broke free from her trance to pick up a porcelain cup off the coffee table and *smash* the mug into pieces on the floor for no apparent reason.

"Why are you breaking stuff?"

"Never been done before, this moment is now new to me. We need change, remember? We've got to alter the cycle." #1 paced back and forth. "What if...the first time around, I didn't get enough sleep? Maybe my clone and me were not as alert for the Easter Sunday blast as we ought to have been. What if you and I go to bed tonight sooner...rather than later?"

"Let's find out," she said with time machine in hand.

"Wait." #1 snatched the glasses away from her. "What

if…our failure is foretold once more?"

"It won't hurt to try."

"Wrong, it *will* hurt! It'll hurt when I'm proven wrong," #1 wailed with a heavy heart. "I don't want to use them anymore. The glasses deject my every attempt. Over and over, I *don't* see any success tomorrow. It hurts my pride to keep seeing myself as a failure. My pride is wounded enough already." As their eyes quietly judged each other, #1 could feel herself shrinking in size from being under her gaze. "Don't look at me like that."

"How do you want me to see you? You told me your pride is wounded."

"Your judgmental stare isn't helping me. I know you are not proud of me. Your eyes are reflecting my pain right back at me."

"I want to help you mend your wounded pride."

"How the heck can I mend wounded pride?"

"Whatever you say, boss. Tell me not to foresee the morning and I won't. If you say it is time for bed, then so be it."

"I doubt we'll ever know what to do."

#1 stood up as if her seat lit on fire, walked past the coffee table, and nearly tripped on the shattered mug. She booted a porcelain shard in anger and, ricocheting off the wall, it nailed the other Hazel's rear end.

"*Ow*, mind my cocoon!"

#1 knew what "cocoon" she was referring to. She became aware of cocoons during her stay in the city. These imaginary cocoons fulfilled necessities. Hazel would enter a cocoon when she left her apartment. Other people's cocoons also became apparent to her. They served as private sanctuaries in public places.

The cocoon had the power to protect. Its shell preserved her pride and she's proud to be humble. She drummed up the glory to glorify humility while in her cocoon.

The dream of outgrowing the cocoon gave her hope. Hope was also given as she grew. She dreamed of giving hope to life beyond her cocoon.

"Funny, I don't recall you mentioning 'the cocoon' at this moment in time. This is a first!"

"I wouldn't have said it if you hadn't nailed me with the shard."

"How ever did I forget about the cocoon?"

#1 slapped her own forehead and sensed a big idea coming on as a whirlwind of thoughts swirled upward in her mind.

"I can feel the answer to our prayers dawning on me." *Eureka*. "Your cocoon holds the missing puzzle piece." She grabbed the original one by the shoulders, shook her, and said: "the solution is you*!*"

"Why me?"

"Because, if I truly am the true leader, then the glasses should show us accomplishing tomorrow's mission." #1 shook her head. "You should be leading *me*, not the other way around."

"You can't expect me to lead the way. I know *nothing* about harnessing the blasts from the Beyond."

"You know enough to be in charge. Remember, you are the original one. You were here first. You're younger than me." #1 bowed her head in shame. "I assumed control ever since I got here, like how *my* elder clone did when I was you, a decade ago. The problem is, knowing more does not necessarily amount to being the better leader. My arrogance is what's blocking our progress. Why is pride so hard to swallow? I mean, there are times when it is okay to have 'healthy' doses of narcissism. However, it is not okay to be a total narcissist."

Her younger self nodded *yes*.

"Before anybody can be able to take charge, they must first do something."

"Do what?"

"Exit the cocoon," #1 said.

BENEFIT OF THE DOUBT

"I'm not ready to shed my cocoon."

"You *are* ready. I've done it, so you can too since we're the same person," #1 said.

"It's easier said than done. Just because I'm able to do it in the future doesn't mean I can do it *now*."

"All you have to do is bless your way through it. *Ah* yes, I can see the blessed cocoon engulfing you." #1 sprinkled pretend fantasy dust on her. "Do you know what I'm doing? I'm giving your cocoon my blessing." #1 danced around her. "Now, you bless it."

"I disbelieve."

"Cocoons do receive blessings. Yours is being blessed

by *others* even as we speak." #1 pointed straight up. "Be one with the blessings. Only by *fusing* yourself with them will you be able leave your cocoon."

The younger one shook her head. "You are trying to define my reality by projecting your delusions on me. Your fantasies about me are not real. *I* am real. Stop projecting falseness on me."

#1, taken aback, stepped back. "I'm only projecting what you'll eventually project on yourself."

"I don't know how to lead us. Can we please stop talking about me?" she asked, wanting to share silence rather than play devil's advocacy with her.

"Let me explain one more thing and then I'll stop pressuring you to lead."

The sweet silence was broken. "*Oh*, alright."

"You already know that the cocoon is for keeping your humble pride safe. But what, pray tell, does it protect your humble pride *from*?"

"I don't know."

"Doubt!" #1 felt a flaming sensation in the middle of her throat. "The cocoon helps you get through the doubt. It shields you from doubts. You also *feed* on it to gain strength when confronting doubt. Life is full of doubt! Tell me, what haven't we any doubts about whatsoever?"

"Nothing?"

#1 shook her head. "The doubtlessly undoubted *does* exist. Once, I tried to itemize the things in life I have no doubts about. I wasn't much older than you are now at the time when I felt plagued by incurable doubt and then it dawned on me: I could make myself feel better by pondering the stuff I have zero doubts about. Doubtless things, you see, can nullify and balance out the doubt."

"What don't you ever doubt?"

"That I will die someday," #1 said with a nod.

"How the heck can that kind of thinking make us happier?"!

"It feels reassuring to be one hundred percent certain about something—anything—considering how much there is to doubt in life. I mean, do you always know what you are doing? No, nobody does. You doubt your abilities. You doubt yourself. You doubt other people. Others doubt you."

"Stop, enough. What are you trying to do? Make me want to end it all?"

"No, I'm trying to make you understand. 'Is it better to die sooner rather than later? Is your life worth living?'

Those sure as hell aren't the kinds of questions you ought to be asking. 'To be or not to be' is *not* the question."

"Then, what is?"

"Doubt, itself, *is* the question. We question it all *because* of doubt. It's what the question is made of." #1 stood up. "I wanted to feel absolute surety. So, I thought about all the things in life I'm absolutely sure of. Death's inevitability is one. If I cut off my little toe, it'd never grow back—that's another. Soon, however, I couldn't think of anymore undoubtable stuff. I started to raise doubts again. I asked myself, 'what about love,' but no, I'm not certain love is *real*. I also don't know if there's an afterlife. I cannot justify faith and even if I do believe, what does *believing* have to do with reality anyway? See? Doubts!"

"Okay, I get it. Death is the only thing we can be sure of."

"No, there's something else we cannot doubt."

"What?"

"It's that we'll *always* have our doubts. If it is not one thing we doubt, then it is another. Doubt will never seize to exist, that's for sure." #1 looked upward. "Why does doubt exist? There must be a reason. Something so absolute must have a purpose."

"I think we need an instinctual awareness of death in order for us to *know* what life is."

"Yeah, much like how doubt can't exist unless the undoubted existed too and since life is undoubtedly mortal, then it can also be said that: if death wasn't inevitable, then nobody would need to have doubts."

The younger one nodded.

#1 said, "Put it this way: if you honestly believed yourself to be immortal, then you would most definitely doubt the one-hundred percent guarantee you got from Death the Grimm Reaper but, by disbelieving in your mortality, you would be lying to yourself too and living a lie. On the other hand, if you believe you'll *always* have your doubts as much as you accept the certainty of death, *then* you would be true to yourself."

"So…we must accept doubt…like how we accept death?"

"Yes, accept! Don't let doubt torture you. Doubt those doubts instead."

"Doubt the doubts." Their eyes seemed to light up.

"Know *this*: it's not just about death. There is a greater purpose. The ultimate reason for doubt is to deliver us."

"I can't shed my cocoon. I'm not able to face my problems without it."

"All you have to do is doubt that doubt."

With fear in her eyes, the original Miss Soffy put on a time machine.

"I believe you," she replied while watching life unfold and at a speed three times faster than real time, their conversations sounded electrified and screechy. "I believe."

The younger one witnessed herself enter the bathroom in fast-forward mode and wash her face. Upon exiting the bathroom in her future, she hit 'play' on the glasses and foresaw herself say to #1, "I've got it! I know what to do."

A SKEWED TIMELINE

*W*hen the hour hand struck "8", making it eight o'clock on Easter Sunday morning, a rainbow-colored aura brightly radiated around the pin-pricking tool.

A minute later, the colorful aura dispersed upwardly to make way for a dark shadow coming from below which rose, spread like black paint, and engulfed the 4-D time-machine charger.

By 8:02 am, the darkness faded away, the tesseract's appearance was back to normal, the underbelly hatch slid open, and out crawled Hazel with a cable running from the time machine on her head to the computer.

When #1 came crawling out shortly after her, they both

coughed uncontrollably, took off the eyewear, and wiped the tears from their puffy-looking eyes.

Crawling out next and following #1 was the *third* Hazel who too rubbed her naked eyes while coughing terribly. She answered to the name "Number Three". The only way you could tell her apart from the youngest one was by the different clothes they wore.

Bringing in "# 3" was the original one's idea. It came to her in the bathroom.

"I've got it! I know what to do." She told #1, "We must reel in one more. You and I are destined for failure. If our mission was a success, then you would not have spent ten years acquiring the necessary knowledge we need to know about the sheep's wool type, the lionesque nuggets, and the toxic web weavers. The *two* of us must fail in order to know how the phenomenon's second coming can be harnessed. However, for us to enlist a THIRD clone from the future would change this *old* story into a brand new one!"

Their weakened limbs buckled and they all collapsed to the cold, hard floor. None of them wanted to talk about their performance in the dome, nor did they desire going over any of the reasons for failing.

They did not wish to discuss their lack of teamwork and held off on complaining about each other. They kept their thoughts to themselves while sprawling out on the floor and eyeballing the ceiling. Taking this breather helped the three Hazels breathe a little easier as the pain in their eyes and lungs subsided.

Looking down from ten feet directly above, she watched her three selves lying there on the master bedroom floor beside the glistening 4-D machine.

Finger flicking the eyewear's off switch, the overhead view of the trio switched back to her present surroundings—she was sitting in the cabin's den with #1 and # 3. After taking off the weighty glasses, she turned to the older Hazels and shook her head in despair at 9 pm on the Saturday.

"I feel so tired," #1 said.

"What's wrong," asked the youngest one.

"Maybe she's simply too old for this. I mean, she *is* ten years older than us."

"No, it's not that. It's like..." #1 sprawled out on the couch. "It's as if something's been draining the will from me for the past hour."

"You mean, ever since around the time Number Three arrived here from tomorrow afternoon?"

"I suppose so, yes."

"What are you talking about? I didn't do anything to you."

"This is all a new experience for me and yet, it isn't," #1 said. "Before you popped in on us tonight at eight, I've always remembered the future to be one involving only my original self and me. For the past hour, however, I've been also remembering how it's we *three* who fail the mission rather than just the two of us. It's as if...new memories are overlapping old ones."

"Yes, we do fail. I just watched us lose tomorrow's battle inside the pin-pricking tool."

"And I saw us lose with my own eyes."

"I did too, ten years ago from what I now recall."

"I don't want to be on the mission all over again," # 3 whined. "When I was the original one, my Number Three tried to talk us out of it, and she obviously failed. Now, you both really should obey me this time around. Hear me when I say: our failure is inevitable. It is time for us to accept defeat."

"Why didn't you and Number One listen to your Number Three when she pleaded to abort the mission?"

3 said, "It's because Number One won't be reasonable and face the facts."

"We already know the future can be altered after it's been foreseen," #1 responded. "As long as the possibility for success remains, however slim our chances are, it is still worth a try. Giving it our best shot is the right thing to do. Listen to me when *I* say: living with the regret of not trying would be even worse."

"See what I mean?"! # 3 *sigh*ed. "It's like talking to a bull up against a brick wall."

"Your skepticism might be the problem." The youngest told # 3, "I too believe we can alter my premonition, if only you would be more supportive and help us wholeheartedly."

While lying back on the sofa, #1 lifted her unusually heavy eyelids to cast suspicious eyes—something about # 3 did not feel right. It appeared as if # 3 was not actually Hazel but, instead an imposter.

Then again, perhaps #1 felt like # 3 had mocked her and she was only reacting to being mocked. Perhaps # 3 was only being realistic. Perhaps #1's suspicion was just her way of dealing with # 3's inability to put heart into the mission. Perhaps.

They had previously discussed tomorrow's strategy. # 3 was tasked with keeping them both standing tall during the invasion inside the 4-D tool. While the youngest one and #1 fought the web weavers in the dome, her duty was to crouch down inside the shaft, hug their waists, and hold them both up like a supportive brace.

In #1's opinion—which she kept to herself—# 3 didn't seem as psyched up as the other Hazel was about playing her role. # 3 lacked gusto and her eagerness to act as their pillar felt faked, which was why #1 had the feeling she would let them down. *You have yet to earn merit.* #1 squinted shrewdly at # 3 and wondered, *why are you not scoring any merit points*?

3 could sense her suspicions but, did she care? No, # 3 had no reason to be concerned about anything.

After all, # 3 was the latest one to arrive—and when you're the last one in from the future, everything that will happen happens in precise accordance with your memories. In other words, when it came to knowing the future, # 3 had the advantage over them both.

They'll never clue in on my ulterior motives. All I must do is keep acting just like the Number Three in my memories, and then everything will go exactly as remembered! # 3 had to turn away from them so that they would not see the carefree and smug smirk on her face.

THE DARK TRIAD

*I*t was a quarter after nine on the night before Easter Sunday. #1 was so tired, she decided to crash on the sofa right then and there in the den. She was still struggling with having two separate timelines of the future running through her head.

A happy memory of two years from today came to mind: #1 was with her decade-older self on a sunny beach in Asia. In that future, they would both be working alongside their dozens of employees—Tara Candido being among them—picking up everybody's litter off the vastly polluted shoreline.

While they both were collecting the garbage by hand, she asked her ten-years-older self, "eight years from now, after fate reels me back in time, will I have regrets about this lifestyle we are living?"

That elder Hazel shook her head. "This is the life."

What happened next was a blur. However, what did pop up in her head were tomorrow's newly recalled memories. #1 now remembered: it was 11:30 am when she felt a chill coursing through her, rushing out the door afterwards for some fresh air, calming herself, looking around at the surrounding forest, and then suddenly coughing up an awful amount of blood.

#1 further recollected how horrified she will be by the sight of her own vomited blood, collapsing on the cabin's front porch, and then afterwards…well, it was unclear what will happen after that—just more fogginess.

In fact, doing any thinking whatsoever about the new timeline created by # 3's presence was only making #1 feel sleepy. *After the web weavers poison me in the morning, do I die tomorrow?* If that be the question, then #1 was not sure whether she wanted to know the answer.

Meanwhile, the other two Hazels were standing in disagreement by the door to the youngest one's room. Although the original Miss Soffy was not as suspicious as #1, she could see how an ordinary person might get to know # 3 and think, *she has an air about her*.

Why are you putting on airs like some kinda stuck-up

princess? "You're the most familiar with tomorrow's events." *And your standoffishness right from the get-go is suspect.* "Just...don't give us poor guidance deliberately, alright?"

3 winced. "*Ouch*, I'm offended. You are wrong about me, I must contend. My heart IS in the mission."

She changed the subject: "It's only nine-thirty. The night is still young. We still have over ten hours to go before the battle begins, and I'm not ready for bed."

"Neither was I when *I* was you at this time." # 3 handed her a time machine.

She shook her head and handed it back. "Won't be needing it."

"Yes, you will. Trust me."

Letting herself in uninvited, she set the eyewear down on the nightstand and then left her original self alone in the room.

At 10 pm, the time-travel device on the nightstand drew her full attention after she had been restlessly tossing and turning in bed.

"I can't force myself to sleep." Her gaze upon the eyewear deepened. "I wonder." She wondered about her purpose in life beyond the mission. What must she do in order to become happy? *What is my purpose?*

There were two ways she could have approached that question.

One way was to keep on wondering. The original one could have wondered about all the goodness which exists. She could live her life as a contributor to the divine.

The other way revolved around the self-interests of the selfish. What if the pursuit of happiness was all about pursuing selfish self-interests? To satisfy everybody's individual desires, then, must be life's purpose and so, our selfish self-interests get placed above all else.

"Being happy is all that matters." *Yes, MY happiness.* Her sense of wonder was devolving. *Happiness for me alone?*

Her sense of wonder was being replaced with a lust for knowledge and when the desire to know took complete control, the snake's temptation had won against the angels' wishes.

The youngest one put on the time machine, cranked its left dial to full throttle, and life sped before her eyes at an exponentially increasing rate. In mere minutes, she had flash-forward shuttled right up to life's end...

The black, white, gray, and snowy static hissed for several seconds before time rewound through her last few minutes alive. A glimpse was caught while going backwards from death.

She's lying down on a lawn. The midday sky looked uniformly drab and motionless. A few hooded figures in crimson robes were milling around in the background. According to the glasses' time gauge, it's her 90th birthday.

'Play' mode engaged and real time kicked in. Hazel had a thick head of white hair and she didn't look as worn with age, for a ninety-year-old, as you might presume while lying there, on the grass in a crimson robe, as the three other robed adults stood around her.

The view of the cloudy sky was blocked by one hooded man who loomed over her and when he knelt, a shadow concealed every facial feature except for the gingery stubble on his chin.

"It's time. Any last words," he whispered in her ear.

The white-haired woman's cracked voice wheezed, "I want the Dark Triad to stay in power."

"She wants the Dark Triad to remain our master," he loudly echoed.

The other two men spoke in unison: "The Dark Triad rules the world!"

Bringing his own face closer to hers, he said, "Right now, our forty-year-old queen is watching us from the past. Hazel Soffy, WE are your most valuable servants. Over the course of your next fifty years, you will become like a goddess to us."

Her younger self felt conflicted. A voice from the heart told her to "stop watching". Even so, Hazel could not help herself and watched on—she wanted badly to *know*.

The tallest and brawniest among them stepped forth to brandish a corked test tube in front of Hazel's face. The strapping man uncorked it and poured its liquid contents down her puckered mouth. After drinking the liquid, she disrobed while lying down and rolled onto her belly.

"Flip to aerial view. Look down at yourself," the big and burly man whispered in her ear.

The Hazel in the bedroom followed his order—she hit a switch on the glasses' rim, flipping the perspective from 'first-person' to 'aerial' view. She started watching herself, lying naked and face-down on the lawn, from ten feet up in the air.

On the ninety-year-old Hazel's back was a tattoo of a solid black triangle with its three points each merging into a poisonous animal. One was a snake. One was a scorpion. One was a spider.

"The tattooed symbol is our flag. Behold the Dark Triad," shouted the man who had yet to speak. He pointed to the scorpion on her back, calling it "the psycho!" He pointed at the spider tattoo and said, "Vellian!" He called the snake "the Narc! The psycho, the Machiavellian, and the narcissist unite as one to form the dark triad! Their toxins are our weapon, for we poison all those who dare oppose us."

"The potion is taking effect. Hazel, look into your eyes as you die. Zoom in on yourself for a close-up," said the first man to the sky when the ninety-year-old *moan*ed.

The dying one rolled over and was on her back again. Having doubts and fears about ignoring the man's orders, the youngest Hazel did as she was told.

Fidgeting with the eyewear's mini controls, Hazel's overhead viewpoint lowered onto her as she wreathed and foamed at the mouth while staring directly upward and, to the forty-year-old, it felt as though eye contact was being made.

Were her wide-open eyes able to see hers looking back? It sure felt that way to the original one.

"Maintain eye contact," she heard one man say.

The elder Hazel's eyes glowed as if they had become twin portholes to a brighter dimension. A few seconds later and in the blink of an eye, those shining eyes turned pitch black—as though her connection to the brightness had been replaced with a darkness all of a sudden.

Her dying last words were meant for not just the ears of the original one: "Oh Dark Triad, behold my vessel who lives in the past. Send my spirit through this temporal link between us. Channel me into my vessel, for I want to serve the dark triad all over again!"

Hazel wanted to take off the time-travel device but, she could not. It was too late for her—she was spellbound by the eye contact.

Every muscle in her body seemed frozen as she lied petrified in bed while being unable to sever their connected stares. The one wearing *the* glasses could not even close her eyes. The white-haired Hazel's darkened eyes somehow spat out the darkness and it *splat*ted against her younger self's peepers.

THE SPLIT PERSONALITY

*T*he original one was lying face up in bed with the eyewear on when she opened her mouth to scream. No sound came out, as if an invisible hand had covered Hazel's mouth—keeping her pinned down and from getting any oxygen for about a minute—until finally, she felt the release of pressure, gasped for air, sat up in bed, and struggled frantically to take off the glasses.

Her naked eyes read the nightstand clock—it was 10:20 pm. Cold sweat beads rolled down her face as she got out of bed to plant both feet on the floor. Her limbs were weak and shaky. *What is happening to me?*

She had been standing upright for only a few seconds before her legs buckled. After she collapsed onto the floor, the bedroom walls seemed to close in on her until the moment when everything went dark.

The doorknob turned at 10:22 pm, her bedroom door opened, and # 3 let herself in. The floor creaked underfoot as she walked up to her younger self who was out like a light and sprawled out beside the bed.

She was not imagining things while lying on the floor. She was neither dreaming nor fantasizing with eyes shut. This *new* bedroom the original one now found herself in was indeed real. It *seemed* like her bedroom, until she looked up—a painting of the Dark Triad emblem now spanned the entire ceiling.

She stared up at the painted symbol of the black triangle encompassed by the snake, the scorpion, and the spider. It looked like the one tattooed on the ninety-year-old Hazel, but what this Dark Triad symbol had that her tattoo did not have, however, was a whitish speck in the center of its triangle.

While glaring up at the off-white dot in the black triangle, the youngest one found herself capable of "zooming in" as if she were operating the zoom function on a camera. The more Hazel zoomed in, the clearer that object became, until she realized what it was. What came into focus were the soles of a woman's bare feet.

"Who's watching me? Is someone else here?" cried the woman standing in the darkness above.

The barefoot woman appeared to be in a place as dark as deep space and yet, she was clearly visible as if somehow, an unseen light source lit up her whole body. From Hazel's zoomed-in viewpoint, it seemed like the barefoot woman was standing only a few feet directly overhead on a clear-glass sheet.

The woman looked straight down as though she felt her stare coming from below. It would later become clear to Hazel who this woman was—she be the other half of her own newly developed split personality!

This "mirror self" of hers, who's standing up above, verged on tears and in anguish she wailed, "Help, I'm in the dark."

"You have on the pajamas I am wearing," she shouted back, but the Hazel down below could neither be heard nor seen by the one who was on the higher level.

When the one up above succumbed to fear and broke down in tears, the other Hazel laughed wildly at her. To see herself in pain and sorrow pleased her for some wicked reason.

She kept on laughing at her and was clearly not herself—the one on the lower plain seemed too sinister to be

Hazel. She opened her physical eyelids to find herself lying on the bedroom floor and looking up at # 3.

"I experienced *exactly* what you are going through," # 3 said.

"I can shut my eyes to see myself in darkness looking like a prisoner."

"*She* is a prisoner, yes. The Dark Triad trapped her."

"Who is she?"

"She's a goody-goody two shoes, worthless, pain in the ass—the other half of our split personality. She would jeopardize our future if she could!"

"I had just foreseen my death and now, all I know is, I don't want my future to change." She got up off the floor.

"In *this* timeline, the mission never gets accomplished—and that is what we want! When you become Number Three by travelling back in time from tomorrow afternoon to tonight, make sure she doesn't alter history by saving Harry's life. We must fail the mission in order to become that ninety-year-old version of us."

"I will become her?"

"Actually, you *are* her," # 3 divulged. "When you both locked eyes, her mind channelled into your body right before she died. The personality you currently have is hers.

What you do not have are her memories because, from right now up until your death, you have yet to experience the future for yourself."

"I get it." The younger one mirrored her smirk. "At the moment of my death, my mind slipped through the time machine and entered the body I'm now in—memories not included!" She gleefully examined her own body in the room's full-length mirror. "I'm back to being my healthy self again!"

"When I was you at this moment in time, *my* Number Three taught me what I'm about to teach you. She showed me some 'motivational' moments in the future, and why we must sabotage the mission tomorrow morning." # 3 looked dead serious. "When it is your turn to be Number Three, make sure your younger self fails to go back in time and becomes the Dark Triad Queen instead. Fulfill my destiny."

The original Miss Soffy was no longer at the cabin in the woods. No siree, the "TRUE" original one was kicked out of her own body on the night before Easter Sunday and sent to a darkly metaphysical prison.

Pitch-black darkness surrounded her, but there was a closed door as dark as her surroundings nearby. She knew it was there because intense light seeped in from behind the door which made the four sides of its rectangle frame brightly visible, and a constant rumbling noise came from outside. She took a few steps closer to get a better listen.

The intense droning sounded like the inner workings of a massive beehive. Hazel had a sinking feeling about the vibe coming from outside as if all of humanity was pressed against the door and she dared not open it.

The Dark Triad Prison appeared to be barren, save for the shut door that had no doorknob and the intensity coming from behind it only added to her feelings of loneliness. She felt as empty as depression.

Only by pushing passed the door could she get out, but whenever her palms pressed against it, she felt painful vibrations. The harder she pushed, the more it hurt and yet, the door would not budge at all.

The one in this prison stepped back and thought, *even if the door could be opened, why would I venture out? I know the scary truth about what is behind this door. The world is mixing and melding into one right outside. Everybody's attitudes and perspectives are all grinding together like the toothy gears of a clockwork machine. If I enter, the machine will only chew me up and spit me out.*

With nothing here to love or be loved by, her lonesome was all she had in dark-triad jail and as the empty feeling sunk in deeper, she got down on her knees.

"My faith is in You," she prayed.

She was getting used to feeling gloomy when a new light source—different from the black door's bright outline—suddenly appeared behind her back. She turned around to see what looked like a movie screen—it was shaped differently from the rectangle screens in movie theatres, though.

This equally large silver screen was more bi-elliptical in shape—like the framed view through binoculars. Colorful lights were projecting onto the big screen and before she knew it, the fuzzy images came into focus to reveal an empty wrestling ring in a bustling stadium.

The so-called "goody-two-shoes, worthless, pain-in-the-ass" do-gooder sat cross-legged in her dark prison to stare up at what looked like a broadcast of an all-star pro-wrestling match.

Overlapping this "show" was a time gauge displayed at the bottom of the screen—much like the kind you would see while wearing Chinn's time machine. The onscreen time gauge read: 8 pm, April 1st, 2019.

PSYCHO THE SCORPION

"First off, I want you to know that Number One is WRONG. Her whole mindset is faulty. It is *not* all about 'being helpful' and 'the collective will'. *My* life isn't about the 'we'! It'll always be all about ME," # 3 said with a nod. "I'll now show you something that you don't already know." She told her original self to "fast forward up to 8 pm on April 1st, 2019".

3 sat beside the number-three-to-be who was lying face up in her bed and wearing the time machine. Using the shuttle dial, she zoomed up to the specified date and time. The play button was pressed and real time kicked in...

The sports stadium bustled with energy. The jumbotron above the wrestling ring was feeding eye and ear candy to the energized crowd. The forty-one-year-old # 3 was seated ringside at the commentators' table with Davey Smits, a pro-wrestling legend.

Davey said to the TV camera, "WOW, what an intense match up! *Phew!* How about a breather and a break? Time for an interlude. We need respite—"

"Check out my wedding ring!"

3 held out her ring finger and the TV cameraman got a close-up on the thick band of pure platinum with its massive diamond fit for Your Royal Highness.

"*Yowza!* Scorpio the Psycho must've dished out big bucks for such preciousness."

"Money is no object when it is 'meant to be'. I've known Scorpio would be my husband for a long time coming. It's all part of the bigger plan."

"I get it. You joined the Big Bang Wrestling Federation a few months ago and called yourself 'MISS' Psycho, but from now on, your name is 'MISSUS' Psycho."

"Davey, just plain call me 'Hazel the Psycho'."

Smits faced the camera.

"Stay tuned, the championship match begins after this recess. Until then, let's look back at what Mr. and Mrs. Psycho did last week."

The jumbotron lit up wildly with sounds of explosions before its screens cut to last week's episode of "The Psycho Ward"—a TV segment where "Hazel the Psycho" interviewed other characters in the professional world of Big Bang Wrestling. The jumbotron showed her sitting by Scorpio's side as usual.

Scorpio the Psycho was a tall wrestler with a broad chest, thick biceps, and he had several scorpion tattoos. The mask he wore even had a scorpion style, as did his attire.

Their set was crafted to resemble a mental institution with a padded room. There was also a booth where a nurse stood behind to hand out pills from. The title "THE PSYCHO WARD" flashed across the jumbotron's screens.

This episode's guests were: Equal Greed—the current Championship Belt holder, and Sloppy—the champ's Haitian masseuse. Equal Greed sat as Sloppy stood behind him.

He wore the belt with pride. The champ's name, "EQUAL GREED", was spelled out across his tight t-shirt. He had Irish blood in him and was among the oldest of wrestlers still wrestling. Even though Equal Greed was shorter than Scorpio, his muscularity made up for it.

Being five and a half feet tall, Sloppy was a scrawny, middle-aged man from Haiti with a white towel slung across his shoulder. Sloppy waited patiently to give Equal Greed a massage and he kept his well-oiled hands hovering near the champ's neck.

"Expect to *lose* the title next week. My husband is the better man and he's going to make you his bleeding bitch," # 3 said with microphone in hand.

"I beg to differ." Equal Greed held up the Championship Belt and roared, "I wanted the title as much as the former champ wanted to keep it, for your information. I didn't want it any more or less than he did. I am Equal Greed. Our wills were the same inside the ring, yet 'twas *I* who won," he reminded them and thumped a fist against his own chest like a confident gorilla.

"Your luck *will* run out," Scorpio replied. "It's time to retire your golden tricks, you old magician. Just walk away and put the title up for grabs. Saving yourself from the pain will only cost you a little embarrassment."

"Nonsense!" Sloppy chimed in.

The champ said sarcastically to Sloppy, "Maybe Scorpio *is* sensible. I mean, who wouldn't want this psycho BOY on their side in a court room, right?"

"Are you denying my physical superiority?"!

"No need to be stronger, younger, and more agility. He

be superior on the *inside!* Equal Greed be for all," Sloppy retorted in his broken English.

"Hush up! Nobody's talking to you, Sloppy," she barked.

"Let the masseuse be heard," the champ insisted while giving Sloppy a high-five.

"Let me tell y'all true. Back home in Haiti, Sloppy be a marathon winner. Sloppy run and run harder than everybody. Sloppy understand the burn-out feeling. Equal Greed spends long-long time in Big Bang Wrestling world." He massaged the champ's back. "Our champion took the long way to get here. The long road didn't make him tired per se, but a happier runner on the path in one great-big marathon. Me? I understand marathons too so, Sloppy understands his marathon." Sloppy had an ear-to-ear grin. "Me gives my best rubdown to Equal Greed."

"I couldn't be here without you, Sloppy. You move me forward at the end of the road."

The # 3-to-be caused a jump cut in the interview segment to see herself shoving Sloppy and *slap*ping him in the face! The crowd below the jumbotron then grew louder all at once and unified roars echoed inside the stadium.

The # 3 to-be sped up the next several minutes. She skipped the part when Hazel joined Scorpio in their spectacular entrance to the ring. Equal Greed's explosive march down the aisle with Sloppy—accompanied by an upbeat rock-and-roll tune—was sped over too. The back-and-forth ("He's now got the upper hand!") exchange between the wrestlers was also fast-forwarded and a half-hour into their gruelling match, she resumed 'play'...

Hazel the Psycho left her seat at the commentators' table. Scorpio was down and apparently unconscious on the mat. Equal Greed had blood smeared all over his face. He crawled up to Scorpio on his hand and knees. The champ mustered his last bit of energy to pin him for the count.

The ref—who was still groggy from regaining consciousness only a few seconds ago—got down beside them and the 1-2-3 count began. He slapped his palm on the mat by Scorpio's pinned shoulder.

"ONE," the ref counted out as Hazel climbed into the ring carrying a folding chair. "Two!" *WACK*, she smashed the chair against the ref's back.

The bell went *ding, ding, ding, ding, ding*! The crowd fell into an uproar.

Sloppy ran up behind Hazel and slung his towel around her neck. The chair dropped from her clutches as she got pulled backwards. She turned around and kneed him in the groin. She pounced on Sloppy and went ballistic on him. She was punching, kicking, hair pulling, face scratching—

you name it.

She tightly gripped Sloppy's throat and squeezed—strangling him with her silky gloves on. It made # 3 laugh wickedly to see him turn blue in the face.

The eyewear raced further ahead until the *whizz*ing halted to show # 3 coming back, from the match, into her private dressing room and locking the door. Hazel the Psycho was now alone.

Right when she flipped the eyewear's perspective to aerial view, Hazel the Psycho finished undressing and bent forward to show the ceiling the tattoo on her back.

The youngest Hazel in the bedroom had a bird's eye-view of the blackly inked triangle—only this time, there was just one, single, lone creature tattooed next to it: the scorpion.

"Being Hazel the Psycho will be a thrill," she said and took off the eyewear smirking.

"It's about THRILLS, yes! First, you'll tattoo that triangle on your back. Next, the tattooed scorpion will magically appear at its left corner while you are throttling and choking Sloppy nearly to death. 'Psycho the Scorpion' will be the name of our scorpion tattoo! We'll have the power to poison others next year." # 3 whimpered in ecstasy. "I just felt a bit of Psycho's power course through me."

The scorpion venom was a tool. Possess it and you'd exude poison. This poison formed a protective bubble. Anybody who'd come into your bubble would feel the venom's effects. Anything they expressed to you would become weak and soft.

You would harden as a result. You'd become callous. Your venomous bubble could weaken people to the point where you'd not even feel them being around.

Those around you would matter less and less. You'd then have less people to compete with. You'd have less people to *share* with. When it came down to having possessions, the Psycho's venom would help you keep what's yours *all* for yourself.

This venom would also poison a certain part of *you*. It'd work away at killing your remorse—an emotion which only *seems* to make you feel bummed.

By possessing the venom, you'd be set free from feeling shame and guilt. The meaning of the word "remorse" would stop making sense to you.

Past wrongdoings would stop being of any significance to you. And then, you'd stop caring. You'd no longer care like how everybody else in the world has to "care". No wonder the Psycho's venom seemed so darn appealing, right?

With it also came the freedom to act whenever and

however you wanted as your behavior would be controlled by impulses. Feeling burdened by social norms? Psycho's toxins had the power to sever all connections with any group.

The need to be considerate for the well-being of others would burden you no more. You'd feel free to behave in any way, even if doing so meant ruining lives.

"If memory serves me correctly, you too are *tasting* a bit of the scorpion power at this time."

Yes indeed, the youngest Hazel *was* feeling a foreign sensation creeping in, and they both looked pleased with themselves.

"Damn right I'm feeling it."

"We're sampling our future and as fate would have it, my destiny is to be the queen of the Dark Triad."

THE ABLE SELF

*T*he other half of her split personality bore witness to everything that the eyewear had shown the youngest one back at the cottage. From her gloomy metaphysical dungeon, she too saw the fresh scorpion tattoo on Hazel the Psycho's back.

The big bi-elliptical silver screen flickered off shortly afterwards, yet there's audio input still coming in faintly—faint voices—as though the sound was not turned all-the-way down.

The other original one walked through the darkness to press her ear against the empty screen and when she did, those voices became clearer—this Hazel was now eavesdropping on their conversation in the bedroom:

"...my destiny is to be the queen of the Dark Triad."

"Wicked, what's next?"

"You're going to see who your life partner will be."

"Whaddya mean? I already foresaw myself married to Scorpio the Psycho."

"Yes, but you'll divorce. We will only *use* him as a steppingstone to snag his brother. You'll be together with his *brother* when the next arachnid gets magically tattooed on your back." # 3 cackled with laughter.

Miss Soffy turned around and faced the shut door. Its rectangle outline looked white hot, making it look scary. Hazel was feeling forsaken in a location which she knew was neither heaven nor hell, seeing as how time's passing seemed too slow for her right now and the afterlife has got to be a timeless place—eternal, if you will. *Time doesn't exist in the afterlife*, she thought. *Time is a reminder of being alive.*

She was not dead, no siree, Bob! So, where was she exactly?

"I must be in a bad dream. I was sent to live in this nightmare while the ninety-year-old me lives in my body back at the cabin." *Who am I?* "I am the TRUE original one. I am the one who rejects the power of the poison. I've been imprisoned for not wanting anything to do with the dark triad."

The droning hum radiating from behind the door was intense enough to make Miss Soffy believe that the noisy world outside might explode her eardrums and Hazel further imagined her retinas being damaged if she did walk out—considering how *blindingly* bright the exit's door frame looked.

While standing before the closed door's white-hot outline in a place as black as pitch, it occurred to her:

"Despite not having a single tool on me to use physically, I might still be able to escape this jail using my three tools of the immaterial kind."

She was talking about her: memories, imagination, and dreams—the three useful instruments that we have all got which nobody can physically take away from us.

"I will rely firstly on my memories and draw from them the power to bust out," she yelled at the scary door.

The one who was confined against her will dug deeply within and recollected the recent conversation she had with Harry Chinn amidst the steam rising from the cabin's frothy outdoor hot tub. He had eased back to let the bubbling water sooth his shoulders.

"What do you do when you don't know what to do," he asked her.

"I guess I... get out my moral compass."

"Where's *my* moral compass?"

"It is located both up above and within you."

"If not north, then where does yours point to?"

"It always points to where my moral fibre is."

"Let me guess, the moral fibre is above us and within us."

Yes, I can see the moral compass pointing to the outside world. There IS moral fibre to be had right outside my damn door. She got down on her knees and prayed, "I know y'all are up there. I am counting on you. Please help me escape from dark-triad jail."

Another memory came to mind suddenly. She remembered what Chinn's pin-pricking tool looked like—its topside, to be more specific. Platinum fiber optics spiralled outward from the center of the flat top on the 4-D construct to form a silvery-swirl pattern.

"Platinum swirls connect us," she uttered toward the heavens.

The "movie" behind her had turned back on and was

flickering. Hazel about-faced to see an array of indiscernible and colorfully blurred images flash across the giant screen again and she grasped the situation.

"Me and my mirror self are about to witness another event."

When the whirling noises came to a screeching halt, the time gauge by the bottom of the flatly rotund and bi-elliptical screen read: 9 am, July 4th, 2021.

VELLIAN THE SPIDER

*T*he glasses took her to see: 9 am, July 4th, 2021. When the play button was hit and real time kicked in, the soon-to-be # 3 foresaw her forty-three-years-old self sauntering through a hall in a luxurious mansion wearing weighty jewellery and nothing else.

The world's most precious metals and expensive stones adorned # 3's naked body in layers and you couldn't see her private parts under the many gem-studded necklaces and belts she had on. The anklets, bracelets, and rings she had were weighing on her too.

She 'paused' the glasses and turned to # 3 who was sitting beside her on the bed.

"How will I afford to live in a mansion and walk around

wearing nothing but decorative treasure?"

"Your constant winnings from excessive gambling will pay for it all."

"*Ah* yes, *of course* I'll be rich. The time machine perfects my life. Premonitions lead me to perfection. The ability to foresee gives me the best possible fate I could ever have. My premonitions create the perfect future for me!"

"*And* thanks to our time machines, there will also never be a better time than the present because every moment I live through amounts to the destiny of my choice. Even this conversation we're having can be defined as 'perfection' since every present moment of mine belongs to the 'perfect' fate I am creating for myself."

She re-hit the play button...

The forty-three-year-old ran her hand along the slick and cold mildew on the stone wall of a torch-lit stairwell as she descended to the mansion's secret underground room. Her jewellery jingled with every step. The cellar's heavy door automatically opened inwardly as she approached and her scantily clad body felt the sucking draft.

Brushing back her windblown hair, she stepped inside and was at once handed a fancy-looking beverage. Candlelight and torchlight reached up to the high ceiling in this windowless room where a royal throne overlooked a dozen adults wearing crimson cloaks.

A pretty man with sex appeal remained at her side as she ascended the steps to the throne.

"Who's that on the steps with me," she asked # 3 after hitting 'pause' on the glasses again.

"Oh, he's the one I told you about—Scorpio's brother. Mach is his name and the business he owns produces and supplies more one-time-use water bottles than any other in North America! You've already divorced Scorpio at this point and Mach is your new lover."

'Play' resumed and she saw # 3 sit on the throne while everybody except for Mach knelt before her—Scorpio the Psycho included.

Mach stood on the steps below her and said to them, "We're gathered here to worship. We must show our thanks for being blessed by her generosity. Let us now bow down at her feet and pray, for she is our goddess…of generosity!"

One of the cloaked men could no longer contain himself and he let a loud *snicker* slip out.

"Who laughed at me?"

3 had heard the snicker and she took offence. The culprit was immediately pointed out by the men standing beside him.

"How dare you disrespect our queen," Mach asked. "My brother must now make you pay. Isn't that right, SCORPIO?"

Scorpio the Psycho grabbed the unsuspecting man from behind, body-press lifted him overhead, and he looked to # 3 for approval before slamming the offender face-first down on the floor, *crack!* The other men's hearts all leapt. Did his neck snap? Was he dead?

Blood gushed from the presumably dead man's nose as he lied there motionless on the floor until the silence was broken with his pain-filled moan, "*Uughh...*" Scorpio clutched the barely conscious man's ankles.

As he was being dragged away by his ankles, Mach looked down at them to say: "We permit you all to live here in our mansion. Heck, Hazel has been GIVING y'all money and if you asked me...she has been too damn generous with no substantial repayment for long enough! Remember the way you were. Y'all were forsaken. None of you can deny how the big city thrives on hating you. Society made you into its toilet! The world would've RUINED all of you if it wasn't for her. Hazel took y'all in and gave you her attention after everybody else had turned their backs. You all owe her like how a stray dog owes its new master."

"Oh, my goddess of generosity, thank you for saving me

from poverty," squeaked a fidgety man.

"Replacing y'all would be easy," he said. "We could hire a smaller and more competent staff to replace you all"— Mach *snap*ped his fingers— "just like that! You are only as good as you are useful in this world and the truth is, you are useless. None of you matter. Life would have tortured you to death if it were not for your goddess. The only thing out there for you is evil!"

"Amen, brother," said the nervous man.

"I'm not your brother. I'm your king," Mach yelled. "For I am her man, and she is your queen."

"My wealth wasn't easy to come by," # 3 said falsely. "Maintaining my income is a constant struggle for me and seeing as how the world hates y'all, none of you are able to help out financially around here."

"Can't you see how great she is for making your lives her burden," Mach asked. "Pray to her if you want to keep the money machine running. Worshipping your goddess of generosity will sustain her will to keep on making the money you need to live on."

Their silence was affirmation enough.

On that morning—after they had been praying to # 3

for close to an hour—the spider tattoo mysteriously appeared by the triangle tattooed on her back and it took its place at the corner adjacent to Psycho the Scorpion. She named it: Vellian the Spider.

MACHIAVELLIAN

From the darkly jail she watched them in the weird "movie" bowing down at her feet and worshipping the one who was, to all intents and purposes, their idol.

"One of The Ten Commandments is: Thou shalt have no other gods! Don't worship a false idol, you spiritless fanatics," she yelled up at the big screen.

3 was using deception to manipulate her subjects. She was dealing in duplicity. # 3 need not be worshipped in order to maintain her cash flow. The money came from knowing the future and yet, Hazel's minions were tangled in a web of lies about her work ethics while the time-travel device was kept as a dirty little secret.

According to Chinn's glasses, they will be persuaded into idolizing her like a goddess and by using them in such a sinful way, the dark triad's second personality gets summoned—the Machiavellian.

As the servants prayed to #3 while she sat on the throne, Vellian the Spider appeared on her back in the same mysterious way Psycho the Scorpion emerged. These arachnid tattoos formed two-thirds of the dark-triad personality—the Machiavellian compliments the psycho.

Being possessed by Vellian the Spider gave her the power to turn people into tools. Those unfortunate enough to be infected with its venom could be used by her and she would manipulate them.

Here's how the Machiavellian poison worked: Vellian the Spider combined three toxins to form its venom. Break it down and you would know the different purposes they each served.

The first toxin would firstly affect your eyes. It could stunt your perception. You'd become blind to people's generous nature. You'd only see everybody's *selfish* side.

You'd then lose hope and faith in everybody. Being poisoned in this way turns you into a cynic. Only when you're cynical *enough* could the second poison take effect.

The second poison would cut the cord between you

and common sense. We're all able to "sense" the sensibility that's commonly shared throughout humanity. We're connected to this sense by invisible, intangible cords which extend upward from our selves.

However, by falling into a cynical state, you'd pay lesser mind to your cord—whereby the second poison then dissolves it, like acid on a rope, while you're unaware.

Your cord would then float back up before you could grab on to it again and you'd have lost your grasp on common sense. And without common sense, your morality would be lost too.

The ones who were possessed by Vellian the Spider wanted everyone's morality to *not* make any common sense and they preferred it if you lost your morals. These Machiavellian people wanted to INVENT morality for everybody.

Vellian made up its own morality whenever it was convenient to do so. It had pragmatic morality. If you were poisoned by it, you'd be swayed by its morality rather than your own. It'd even manipulate you into believing an immoral action to be moral.

Machiavellian people want to *use* us as if we're disposable, cheap goods. Without freewill, there would be no antidote to their toxicity. Your freewill fights to keep you from being manipulated by a Machiavel.

The main purpose of "freewill" ought to be to let us reach our potentials. Human potential, mind you, is kept and housed within common sense. And your potential will not bloom unless it's free to roam the realm of common sense. And only within common sense do we realize our full potentials.

There's always potential in you. It can always be reached. This power and glory can always grow within us all. There's power and glory in freewill. A Machiavellian person, on the other hand, sees freewill as one's worst enemy.

The third toxin acted as a blocker. It could block you from reaching back up to common sense so that your freewill would be kept out of reach. This poison would prevent you from tapping into freewill! And consequently, without freewill, your true potential stays dormant.

IMAGINATION

She walked up to the shut door in the darkness. She wanted out. Her bare soles found some traction on the smooth floor. With braced footing, Miss Soffy pushed against its vibrating surface as hard as she could but, the harder her palms pressed, the more it hurt.

The stabbing pain in her hands was becoming unbearable. Unable to take it anymore, she let out a *scream,* flung herself a few steps backward, and stood hunched over with her hands on her thighs while panting heavily.

"Dreams, imagination, and memories—the three tools I still have on me to make my jailbreak with," she said in solitude. "My memories have reminded me to get in the right frame of mind when it's gloomy. Yeah, I must keep my wits about me. And now...*imagination* will help me push onward."

After pondering for several minutes, she finally imagined her very own extra-special version of a railroad locomotive. Her mind's eye could see its engine's inner workings.

The big driving wheels were held together and driven by rods. The cylinders pushed the pistons to-and-fro to keep on cranking the wheels.

Lightning fuelled this train, and an extra-special kind of "willpower" generated the lightning. The willpower working here worked in the same way as a seesawing railway handcar.

She imagined this seesawing handcar to be within the engine. Hazel further pictured herself to be inside one of the train's compartments and she could feel the willpower while barrelling along the tracks at high speed.

She felt a deep longing and a strong urge to walk with Him in His kingdom. This heavy pining was what kept on pulling the handcar's arm *down*.

While at the other end of the walking beam was the *dream* of being "here" with The Messiah. Wishing for The Messiah's arrival kept on pivoting the arm back *up*.

Those two wills pulled up and pushed down—like two

passengers operating a seesawing railway handcar—to keep the lightning generators in the engine cranked.

The whole engine glowed brighter as the locomotive picked up speed and it kept on accelerating until she finally imagined the bright light to be all that there was.

She kept in mind the imagined train. She believed in it. She took a deep breath, exhaled, stepped right up to the scary door in the darkness, and pushed.

The needling pain intensified in Hazel's palms as she kept on pressing on the door while her legs pushed against the ground, which added more push to her pushing hands, and she pressed harder and harder against its hurtful surface even though it hurt like the dickens—all the while thinking, *I WILL get outside!*

NARC THE SNAKE

*T*he third and final poisonous critter surfaced as a tattoo to take its place at the last remaining point left vacant on her tattooed triangle. The newest symbol was of a snake and its narcissistic character unified the two other tattoos to complete the Dark Triad—the narcissist complemented the Machiavel and the psycho.

Psychotic traits, Machiavellian behavior, and narcissism—they be the three personality disorders that formed as one to bring into fruition the character of the dark triad.

The tattoo slithered onto her back sometime between the pillow talk and the throes of passion she shared with Mach while lying under the king-size ceiling mirror in the well-lit master bedroom of their mansion around thirteen hours after Vellian the Spider came on the scene. That snaky symbol for narcissism was called Narc the Snake and it concluded the Dark Triad trilogy tattooed on # 3's back.

Hazel was at war with the narcissists in the big city. They kept on attacking her imaginary cocoon in order to make themselves feel superior.

She learned a thing or two about narcissism and had gotten to know the nature of the narcissist better while their narcissistic toxicity was bombarding her cocoon—and like the G.I. Joe cartoon characters used to always say every Saturday morning: "and knowing is half the battle!"

The # 3 to-be in the bedroom watched her future-self inherit the snake venom on the night of July the 4th, 2021, and inheriting its power felt intoxicating yet sobering at the same time.

The snake venom was a tool. Anybody possessed by it could exude poison. The poison worked well at weakening other people's defenses.

With it, we could come exploding in on others, or we might creep in on them slowly and quietly. Either way, with the poison as our tool, other people's boundaries would seize to be an issue for us.

Above all else in the world, there's competition. Wouldn't you agree? We must be better than our competitors in order to succeed. Being *better* than them means they're *worse* than us and we'd poison everybody with our venom to make ourselves the best.

The poison worked well at shrinking the willpower in others. Thus, the narcissists kept on lashing out at competitors until their poison eventually shrunk the competition down to a beatable size.

The snake venom was a tool for relieving the pain and woes of *envy*. Who be worth envying while your venom makes *you* better than everybody else? Nobody! There would be constant smirks on our faces if we were possessed by Narc. We would be constantly *sigh*ing smugly with relief too.

3 accumulated worldly possessions by using her venom on the world until the day she physically died. Whenever opportunity knocked, she was ready to take advantage of others for selfish reasons.

She would be unable to always get her way and take more and *more* away from everyone if it were not for the venom's onward push from within. The poison's power was in her blood. She inherited its power like how your parents' genes are inherent in you. The snake venom was like her birthright.

We have all got birthrights. Some have been bestowed family fortunes while others were born with different rights. Does that mean life should revolve around our birthrights? Does the world owe you in accordance with your birthright?

If so, then that means you were not born to *be* a somebody. No, you were born to *have!* The world owes us what we're each born to have! Wouldn't you agree? So, why worry about *being* anything for anyone, right?

"I'm not indebted to the world in any way," # 3 insisted. "The world owes *me* everything! I owe the world *nothing!*"

She had the most grandiose sense of entitlement thanks to her venom. # 3 thought, *I am entitled to the world and everything in it because of my abilities granted by the venom and the eyewear.*

During the ninety-year-old's reign as the Dark Triad Queen, there had been people who tried to shame her.

"Who're they to stand between me and what I want? They've no right to call me a narcissist," she'd tell herself in anger—angry from being shamed.

Fortunately for # 3, Narc's power made her immune to shame. She could easily deflect any blame. Her inner snake was a shield against the feelings of guilt.

The narcissistic Hazel, who knew no remorse, once muttered to a stranger on the street: "I don't deserve my riches, you say? Damn your jealousy! It is not *my* fault you are the lesser one between us. All you are to me is a tool anyway. If I can't exploit you, then you don't exist to me. I really don't care what you or anybody else thinks. You *all* attack me out of envy."

She derived much pleasure from how well the time machine complimented her toxins. *Finally, I am above everybody else,* she would think.

It's lonely at the top, though. She was not blind to how having advantages sets her apart from the disadvantaged. There would always be a rift between her and the soulful hearts of everyone else.

To compensate for feeling isolated from most others, # 3 found assurance, comfort, and entertainment in her own mind's "magic". She had begun to think that the magical thoughts of everybody else were "bullshit!"

To Hazel the narcissus, the only magical thoughts worth thinking about were her own. # 3 depended *too* much on her own "magical thinking" and she grew to despise the company of others.

"The Dark Triad let me sample its yummy power at this point in time, as a reminder. So, you too must be tasting Narc's strength right about now."

"Mm-hmm," *moan*ed the # 3 to-be in ecstasy.

"I see. Now I know, and knowing is half the battle," said the one in dark-triad jail to the big screen.

3 said onscreen, "Narc is named after the mythological Narcissus. You know, the character who drowned while trying to embrace his own reflection shimmering on the surface of deep waters." They both smirked smugly in the bedroom. "Nark the Snake is a king! Long live the Snake," were her last words before the strange movie screen vanished and the dark surroundings got even darker.

THE FOURTH OF JULY IN 2021

*T*he forty-three years-old Hazel was lying on her scarlet red bedding while facing skyward and admiring herself in the ceiling mirror. Mach scuttled onto the bed on all fours to hover over her like a cat as she full-bodily swooshed and swished the silk sheets.

Mach's fingers caressed her face. In her eyes, he was drop-dead—handsome enough to be a dead ringer and pass for the mythological Narcissus himself. Their faces pressed together, and they open-mouth kissed madly for several long seconds before he let gravity drag him to her.

"My chest feels the heat coming from yours."

"You're so very hot blooded too," she responded (at 10:10 PM).

"I burn for you like a torch, my hotness."

"*Oh* yes, you *torch*…*torture* me…*!*"

Meanwhile, 'twas twelve hours ahead in the Philippines where Tara Candido lived. Tara was telling time—it was 10:10 AM—when she noticed through the opened door a mini school bus stopping near her driveway.

She stepped out and was on the front porch hand-wave signalling for the driver to *please wait*. Not wanting to keep everybody on the bus waiting, Tara hurriedly looked all around the first-floor unit in search of anything she might have forgotten to pack—this nice lady did not want to leave her humble abode unprepared today.

Tara's big handbag giggled jingly as she rushed outside. The door on the bus swung open for her. She was the driver's last pick up, making it a dozen carpoolers in total—all of whom were bureaucrats over forty years old.

She was an admin bureaucrat, a front-line desk clerk for the Department of Recycling Intake—whose job it was to oversee the volunteers reporting in for every shift. Tara worked at the same office location in the *same* full-time position for a whole year straight.

The bus jolted onward, causing Tara to stumble and fall onto the nearest available seat. Sitting across from her was

Mr. Morales, a man with an accounting career for the government.

A mutual friend introduced her to Mr. Morales last year at a dinner party and he was the one who brought Tara in on the "secret". Its funding was already green lit when they both met and even though it was not *his* brainchild, if not for Morales's accounting skills, the project probably would not have seen the light of day.

Minus the driver, everybody else on the bus outranked Tara in the food chain of bureaucracy. They were all higher-up senior admin officials in both the public and the private sectors.

Tara reached inside her handbag and pulled out a clipboard. The clouds parted to let the morning light shine in through her window and onto the simple word equation written on the clipboard's paper which read: LIFE = LOVE = TRUST = FAITH, and nothing more.

"Is that for the class," Mr. Morales asked, pointing to her clipboard.

An unhappy *sigh* was her first response.

The bus passengers were given homework last night to be graded later today. These bureaucrats were each given a sheet of blank paper and told to "complete it" like they would a form. The assignment stumped Tara.

"How do I fill out a form that has no questions or instructions?"

Her question was left unanswered, and no other instructions were given. All she had to go on were her heart and guts. Tara's organs simply told her to write on the blank page: LIFE = LOVE = TRUST = FAITH.

"You'll see my homework when everybody else sees it," Tara told him.

LIFE = LOVE = TRUST = FAITH. Last night she realized, *I am most alive when I feel love. Love is the same thing as trust. To trust is to have faith. Having faith thusly equals being alive!* Tara's philosophy seemed so grand yesterday but today, not as much so.

The others probably wrote down specs, stats, analysis reports, and proposals necessary for the project's development. *Surely, they had been practical and pragmatic about it. I bet they are going to make me look foolish.* Tara twisted around in her seat to scan the others on the bus and thought, *my simplistic equation stinks.*

Her whole body felt like it was shrinking in size. She faced forward and sunk back down as if her seat turned into quicksand.

Wasn't her insecurity and self-doubt justifiable? Tara knew herself well enough to know that she was *not* perfect.

She was neither smarter nor more attractive than everybody else. She doesn't dominate. She's not the best. Not only did Tara find it difficult to accept herself now, but there had also been many times in the *past* when she would struggle in vain with her self-esteem.

What made Tara feel better about herself was a saving grace. Her saving grace was the fact that nobody else on earth *is* her. *I am a 'one and only' version of myself*, she thought with a smile while staring out at the moving scenery.

Grace Seaver sat at the back of the bus and was on the police force before she got married. "The Archive" was *her* brainchild, and it had full backing from a secret club for scientists.

The bus was taking them way out into no-man's land where those secret-science leaders had a base stationed. "The Archive" was the code name for an operation to bureaucratize a secret taskforce tasked with defending, on all fronts, from foreign corruption.

The group had twelve members and the name of this "band" was: The Archive. The Archive oversaw and supervised artificially-intelligent beings living in a prototypical world—a virtual simulation created by the computers at the scientists' South Asian hideaway.

Mrs. Seaver's husband was the secret club's one-thousandth member and Grace had gotten to know nearly all his fellow members better socially since the day he was sworn in around seven years ago.

Yes, Grace Seaver was the one who dreamed up the "The Archive", but it was the spirits of generosity who kept the entire operation afloat. From nothing—out of thin air—The Archive was formed, all thanks to "the spirits of generosity". *They* were ultimately its true founders.

Mrs. Seaver had the will to fight like a hero for the sake of generosity after those spirits came to her in a dream one morning. Grace became a "David" while her "Goliath" was the "bureaucracy" of the scientists' secret society.

This bureaucracy she and her husband found themselves in was formidable. Made from unfeeling logic and cold calculations, its inflexible rules did not have loopholes and every time she proposed The Archive operation, red tape bound her even when some club members found the project to be compelling.

The scientists were all bureaucrats at heart. And bureaucrats have no choice but to ignore their own *personal* judgments whenever dealing with official matters.

The system cannot see the meaning of anybody's life as we all be not special in its eyes, and it has no favorites—

even when you deserve to be one. The bureaucracy turned them each into nothing more than a number assigned to a case, you see.

Grace's challenge was to make her case shine so bright that she would not be ignored. She got the backing for The Archive by stirring up the hearts and souls of them all into a mix to create a "chemistry" from their generous natures and *that* was called "generosity fusion".

Grace Seaver did not actually "create" the generosity fusion per se, for it had always been around and present as a secret treasure hidden from the five senses until *she* unveiled it.

Grace shed a light on all the generosity we have kept hidden away. She made generosity fusion accessible to everybody in her husband's club so that we ALL might bask in the radiance of the scientists' generous will, someday.

Generosity fusion generated the multi-million dollars needed for financing The Archive. The Archive *was* the mission—and the mission was to bureaucratize an artificially-intelligent taskforce for the purposes of learning how to defend ourselves from foreign corruption on all fronts.

With Grace's guidance, the secret scientists became affiliated with financiers who backed the bureaucratic development of the artificial intelligence within their virtually simulated prototype of society. The paying sectors, both private and public, were all given "Karmic insurance" by the secretive scientists—meaning every contribution to The Archive would *faithfully* come back around and greatly benefit each contributor in one way or another.

Grace Seaver shed a light on how the generous nature in us all fuses together which, in turn, strengthened the contributors' generosity. Generosity fusion may have been forgotten but, it's not gone.

The people who fused with generosity gained the power of attraction, seeing as how their observations became more attractive to all. Their individual observations were *fusing* together to shine freshly new outlooks back out upon the environment and this "fusion" was attracting other people's thoughts and feelings like a magnet.

When the scientists and financiers fused with generosity, not only did they all become more attractive in everybody's eyes, but their powers of observation also got keener. They were able to "see" the observations of others more abundantly clearer than ever before, and this "observation attraction" kept the generosity fusion in the people's eyes.

The dozen bureaucrats on the bus were going to the club's secret base where they could play like gods and be paid handsomely to protect the fictional, yet self-aware, citizens in their computer-generated community—protecting the artificial intelligence from corrupting foreign characters programmed to import corruption, that is. They were the twelve who operated the "superhero" characters in the virtual reality.

Tara turned to face the rear window of the bus when Grace caught her attention. She gestured for Tara to come sit with her and so, they sat beside each other for a little chat.

As they were chitchatting, Tara wondered, *why was I chosen?* After all, Tara did feel inferior to everybody else on the bus. They all had more experience, skills, education, and entitlement than her. Grace's feet attracted her gaze.

"We both know you could've hired somebody else who has a lot more experience, skill, education, and entitlements than me. I am not worthy compared to some of the other applicants. So, why did you pick me," Tara asked with eyes downcast.

"We need *you.* Our team must keep on growing up if The Archive is to be a success. You spark growth spurts from us like nobody else can. Do you remember when I interviewed you? I asked if you've ever felt any growth spurts at work."

Tara Candido had not forgotten the odd question which in turn refreshed memories of many gruelling hours spent behind a desk right outside the portable offices on the mount overseeing a shipping yard in the Philippines. Tara's time at the Dept. of Recyclable Intake was "boring" to say the least.

She had the *same* duties to do every workday. Day in and day out, Tara sat at an outdoor desk to liaison between the foremen she faced and the department chiefs who backed her.

Growth spurts? *Huh?* The question ought to have been: *How badly did working at the D.R.I. stunt my growth?!*

The question made Tara recall noticing some volunteers looking like they were feeling rejected and dejected at the outdoor desk counter after waiting in line for quite a long time.

Tara once saw a woman with a brightly beaming face standing in line who later had her smile turned upside down when she was told: "you didn't do the form right this time around. Come back after you do it again."

Was hope being ruined whenever "a deserving earner" got denied at the counter? Tara wanted to make the deserving earners feel accepted even though the bureaucracy could not let her.

Either submit the correct and right stuff or else your application gets denied. No room for deal making within the bureaucratic process. Only the facts matter, nothing else. Tara could give nobody a little slack no matter how much they deserved some in her eyes.

The question made Tara recall the times when she tried to move the lineups along more quickly. She would work extra hard at processing the people as fast as possible. She soon discovered how futile it was to work speedily in a bureaucracy. Lineups only seemed to grow *longer* the faster they moved along.

Tara also noticed how, the faster she processed the people, the angrier did everybody seem to get. From aggressive attitudes do conflicts arise but, when it came to slower-moving lineups, the people settled into a zombie-like state. Bureaucracies prefer zombies. Zombies do not get uppity, and she felt as if life was a bureaucratic process even outside of her workplace.

"Life is one lineup after another," she told Grace on the bus. "All I do is go with the flow and mind my own business, like how we wait in line for our turn with our heads down, and usually, there is somebody at 'the counter' telling me why I don't deserve approval for some darn reason. I also notice the people in line before and after me who *do* get approved. It seems to me like they have got it made, whereas I do not. No, *I* get sent to the back of another lineup. What happens when somebody finally *does* approve my application? I *still* get ordered to go join yet another lineup, that is what! LIFE is moving me along. Can't *I* ever be the one who is moving life? No, I cannot. *Nobody* can change the situation while waiting in line. You know what happens when we step out of a lineup? We lose our place in line! All we can do to keep ourselves from 'losing out' is stay in line and let the whole process turn us into zombies. No wonder there are so many zombie movies and zombies on TV. Art reflects life, Grace."

"The same can be said about vampires, Tara. Vampires are the reason we keep to ourselves in the lineups. Attract too much attention to yourself and you'll eventually be seen as being *food* or even worse, somebody to hate. Some people out there have bloodthirsty minds, make no mistake about it. They are not interested in joining you in going along with the flow. These vampires have the desire to rip you apart! Keeping yourself in line with your head down keeps you safe from the bloodthirsty. We don't want them to rip apart people like you."

"Growth spurts?" The question made familiar faces in the lineups at work come to mind. "Come to think of it, recognizing a person amidst strangers *has* made me feel like I'm going through a growth spurt" was Tara's answer during her job interview.

Tara would be looking out at the crowd from behind the counter when she would see somebody in the lineup who was here before. They had come in the past only to be denied by her department. They were probably told to "redo their form and come back".

Seeing the familiar face sometimes sparked an internal flare which caused her to feel like she was physically growing. Sometimes it was not a face, but a voice.

She was not sure how to describe the reason for those growing pains. Tara imagined an invisible, intangible cord running, from up above, down to her head's crown and she believed a "strumming" happens when the sense of familiarity arose between people.

Whenever the familiarity clicked in, not only inside the mind but also in the heart and soul, the "cord" gets strummed. The strum vibrated down the cord, entered Tara's body through the crown, and aroused her growth spurts.

"Yes Grace, I haven't forgotten the growing pains caused by the growth spurts."

"Keep on remembering. Your new job depends on growth spurts."

There they both were, sitting next to each other on the mini school bus in the Philippines. Tara looked out the rear window to notice a physically fit, six-foot tall, two-hundred-pound bald man with red skin running after the bus at a superhuman speed and consequently, it was right then at that very same moment when the Dark Triad Queen—aka # 3—had a spastic bodily reaction as her skin dripped with sweat from the throes of passion and she impulsively shoved Mach's sweaty body off the bed to his surprise. There *they* both were, lying naked and exhausted inside the mansion while the Fourth of July fireworks lit up the night sky in their view from the bedroom window.

Meanwhile, the mini school bus was being attacked in broad daylight by the demon whom Hazel had nightmares about while city-dwelling a few years back. Its six-yards-long tongue shot out at the bus's rear window like how a toad can snag a passing fly.

Grace and the other passengers too were seeing the hairless demon-man with crimson skin as it caught up to the speeding minibus and Tara joined in on the group screaming when its whip-like tongue *smash*ed through the rear window.

Its flailing tongue managed to wrap around a seated bureaucrat and using him as an anchor, it reeled itself in. It tore the emergency back door off its hinges using superhuman strength.

It now wreaked havoc inside the little school bus. The panicked driver got transfixed on what was dead-ahead as he intuitively put the pedal to the metal.

"EVERYBODY HOLD ON TIGHT TO YOUR SEATS," the driver shouted as the bus gunned it at top speed right before he cranked the steering wheel to make the sharpest turn possible while slamming on the breaks and the tires *screech*ed—*CRASH*!

Reports of this school bus crash in the Philippines was on the news later that day. The media reported how the minibus was found: off the side of a country road, facing the wrong direction, and with its totally mangled rear compressed against a tall boulder protruding from the earth.

The passengers all claimed that a man in red body paint had run faster than the bus could go, caught up to it, ripped the back door off its hinges with his bare hands, attacked them using a whip-like weapon, and caused the crash. However, if there really was such a man, then he left behind zero evidence of his presence.

Hazel's nightmarish man-demon was nowhere to be found because it disappeared a split second before the crash—for it had to react fast: either teleport back to its layer underneath the physical plane and remain unharmed or go through the torture of being flattened between the bus's metal and the rock. Sufficed to say, it chose not to suffer.

Among the thirteen people on the bus, there was one fatality: the driver. Further investigation later concluded he died of a heart attack while unbuckling his seat belt and attempting to exit the wrecked vehicle.

It was unhappy with the death toll. The hellish freak stupidly wanted *more* death and desiring deaths is as terribly wrong as wanting children to overrun the world. Yes, it was a very horridly bad thing indeed.

The moment it sprouted from underneath the material world was precisely when # 3 acquired the third type of dark-triad venom. Her tattoo's magic completion was what enabled it to surface. Attacking the bus passengers who acted as spiritual beacons in the Philippines was its first order of business.

Its attack on Tara Candido *was* a coincidence. Along this timeline, Tara never made a commercial for nor picked up beach litter with Miss Soffy, but she might have recognized her on TV in the Big Bang Wrestling episodes as Hazel the Psycho was indeed a fan favorite.

It very wrongfully hated the defenders against foreign

corruption on all fronts—hating them for choosing to follow the spirits of generosity. It misjudged the bus passengers—putting the liberal bureaucrats in the same category with everybody else and indeed seeing them *all* as insignificant nobodies.

The man-demon failed to notice the meaningful significance of the fight for foreign anti-corruption. It also failed to see any significant meaning to the bus driver's life.

Over time, the bus driver would've developed friendships during the routine rides he was scheduled to give Grace Seaver and his other eleven passengers. He would have been happy to learn more about The Archive if his heart had restarted before it was too late. He indeed would have, yes, in time.

EASTER SUNDAY

1 got out of bed feeling determined. She was going to go through with the mission this morning, no matter what. That decision was already made up in her mind and she saw no point in watching what will happen after the cosmic blast surges through the pin-pricking tool at 8 am.

At 6 am, the three Hazels were sitting in the cabin's den holding steaming coffee mugs and the chirping birds outside were filling the silence between their sips and slurps.

As they quietly enjoyed their early-morning coffees together, #1 was imagining a locomotive's caboose running at full steam. Where was it backtracking too? Her answer: the past—for only in the past could Harry Chinn be saved.

"What's on your mind," # 3 asked #1.

"Wouldn't it be interesting to remember the earliest moment when body and soul first became one—the spark at life's starting the point—the moment of BIRTH? I mean, could a person even ever recall that far back?"

"The more pressing question is whether or not we foresee what will happen in two hours," the youngest chimed in.

3 already knew the *final* answer to the original Hazel's question and so, she lied to both of their faces.

"In *this* timeline, we *do* fast forward to 8:02 am," # 3 said and shook her head. "Like I told you both last night: the outcome was shown to us before our battle, and we failed nonetheless."

The good night's rest had lifted the fog in #1's head. She could now recall the future moments prior to and after the mission—#1 remembered this exact conversation they were now having about whether to foresee their inevitable failure with the eyewear or not.

"Then it's settled. We go on faith alone and decide against foreknowing," #1 decided. "We must do the opposite of what Number Three did at this time when she was you."

"I concur."

"Me too. This cycle I'm in can't be altered without change and the only way to get on a new timeline is by doing differently from what fate had dictated," said the youngest.

It was at 11:30 am on this Sunday when #1 first felt the chills coursing through her whole body. She then rushed out the door for some fresh air, calmed herself, looked around at the surrounding forest, and suddenly coughed up an awful amount of blood!

#1's memory of later today further recalled how shocked and horrified she'll be by the sight of her own vomited blood. #1 would then collapse on the cabin's front porch and soon afterwards...well, it was unclear what happens after that—just nothingness, as though #1 no longer existed.

If "to be or not to be" really was the question, then #1 apparently chose "not to be". She did NOT want to die per se, for desiring death is as horribly bad as wanting children to overrun our lives.

What #1 wanted was the mission's success, and she would choose to go down fighting for it rather than throw in the towel.

#1 had awoke feeling sick and tired. You might say she

got up today with her head in a bad place.

#1 was thinking about the bullies who overrun and overcrowd the lives of everyone. She was sick of them having the insolent and impudent audacity to disrespect the worthy, and their wilful ignorance in the face of discernment made her want to puke.

#1 was tired of the bullying between the rich and the poor—how they choose to resent each other rather than appreciate one another. She was also fed up with being overrun by the con artists who bully and take advantage of the performance artist in us all.

Instead of having faith, she had distrust in the big city—and the fear the bullies spread was to blame.

I cannot take the bullying anymore, she thought while sitting quietly in the den with her two younger selves.

3 said to the youngest one, "You'll go back in time this afternoon as opposed to ten years from now. You will become Number Three. You'll no longer become Number One, which means neither will I. Ten years from now, I do NOT pop into the past to relive last night. It is because of the alignment problem. Number One was a specific age when the device reeled her in from 2028 to the present. On the contrary, at the exact moment in 2028 when the original Hazel time travels to the past, I will be sixteen hours

older than Number One was. I will not be the same age as Number One at that precise point in time. In other words, my age doesn't align correctly with the fateful moment the glasses turn the original Hazel into Number One."

#1 nodded and added, "Number Three can remember your future, but not me. I have no memory of your futures, just like how the eyewear won't show *my* lifespan to you both. It appears as though I'm now living a separate life and neither of you are the original me." #1 *sigh*ed. "My *true* original self is either existing sixteen hours in the past or, she...no longer exists at all."

#1 walked over to the 4-D tesseract in the master bedroom. It fascinated her.

"It doesn't matter what the eyewear will show us because the now determines the future and presently there is HOPE. Yes...me, myself, and I WILL win the fight against the toxic web weavers this time around," #1 thought aloud confidently.

PROPELLING DREAMS

*T*he other half of the youngest Hazel's split personality stuck in dark-triad jail was on all fours and her hands still felt the pain from pressing so firmly against the pitch-dark door's magically defensive surface. She stood up, brushed herself off, did a twirl in her pajama gown, and hoped for escape.

She had previously watched her future-self living luxuriously on the prison's big screen and was feeling guilt-stricken. Her other personality deserved shame.

3 ought to have been ashamed of herself for caring more about her amassing bank account than she did the moral, the virtuous, the ethical, the equitable, and the just beyond-a-reasonable-doubt people across the lands.

She reminded herself: "Instead of earthly possessions, I'd rather my worth be defined by my REPUTATION. My brain wants to manipulate the future, yet my heart wants otherwise. I believe in seeking a future that's set *free* from our manipulative ways," she confessed to whomever might be outside listening in.

She disliked her other half for being a selfish self who'd take advantage of the present whenever she pleased and without the authorization. The one who needed a jailbreak need not the premonitions in order to prepare herself—faith alone did well enough at keeping her prepared for a life well-earned.

She started bellowing at the locked exit like a banshee, desperate for some passerby to hear her siren of shame and come busting through from somewhere outside. It did not take long for Hazel to get tired of yelling and quietly come to grips with her remoteness—rescuing herself was the only option.

"Of my three tools—the memories, the imagination, and the dreams— there's still one tool I have yet to use: the dream drummer-upper," she remembered.

She referred to the people who had a knack for recalling their sleep-induced dreams as "the dream drummer-uppers". Being capable of reflecting on them too—to also have the dream drummer-upper ability—made her feel proud.

She massaged her sore hands while thinking back on recollected dreams, calling to mind fuzzy visions—some contained fears and others regret.

Miss Soffy had a dream where she was about to get off at the next underground rail station. The train stopped and it dawned on her as she was alighting, *that important thing is left behind where I was sitting, oh no*—and the sliding doors closed, squishing her almost to death.

Another dream of fear she had involved what looked like a rat terrier with light brown patches and short ears. Hazel took the collarless and cute dog into her home in the dream and when she did, little rodents came following next like the mice and rats led by the pied piper. She later surmised it to be about the necessary fear of that which attracts unwelcome company or unwanted things.

She remembered a hazy dream of a handicapped man sliding down a playground slide on a wheelchair—and yes, how he got his chair up there to begin with is indeed another mystery altogether.

Hazel stood by the bottom of the slide when the man in his wheelchair slid down and regretfully, she missed her chance at catching him before he hit the ground. Reflecting on it made her sad as dreams of regret usually do.

Her mind's eye looked back on the dreams of taking school exams and tests in a classroom. Hazel did not know it yet, but there's something to be said about those sweat-inducing, school-related dreams—which she'd learn later on this Sunday morning.

By drowning, in a fire, under gunfire, or being frozen solid and shattered to icy pieces—she recounted some ways to dream of dying, and even though this was indeed a dark topic, brooding on it did get her adrenaline pumping no less.

The dreams were the blocks for building self-confidence, and she made a particularly vivid one the spearhead of her morale. She called it: "the banquet table pre-show dream."

In it, she took a seat at a long dinner table where several unfamiliar faces were already seated. She noticed the tablecloth was purple and the spotlessly clean plates and cups, set before every guest, were all empty—the nourishment and sustenance had yet to be served.

While waiting for the feast, they shared their patience with her, and Hazel felt tranquilly blissful right up until she awoke.

While considering the dream's meaning, she stood tall, turned around to face the mystery behind the door, and squinted her eyes at the only light source around: the black door's intensely bright rectangle outline.

She imagined that the dining room table from the dream was right outside her door. *Everyone is waiting for the feast to commence and yet, they don't want to start without me*, she thought—about the dream. *But it is not only me they are waiting for. Ultimately, we are all waiting for our host or the guest of honor to arrive—the one who'll sit at the head of the table.*

"I've accepted my invitation to the upcoming banquet." She kept on backing away from it. "More guests are arriving to sit with the others, and I must join them. I refuse to miss out on the patience they are all sharing out there without me. I must bust out of here to fulfill the dream."

The shut exit was now around ten yards up ahead. "The virtue of patience compels me," she shouted and ran full-steam straight ahead while keeping in mind those weighty dreams spearheaded by the banquet table pre-show dream and *wham!*

She had shoulder-rammed the door with all her might. Her back was on the pitch-dark floor. A new pain spread through her shoulder and arm.

She turned to look at the closed door and, low and behold, it had budged! Slightly more outside light and noise seeped in through the crack—she had rammed it open wide enough for her fingers to squeeze through.

"Even though they don't want to dine without me, I mustn't keep them waiting at the table for much longer. After all, patience does wear thin."

Hazel poked four fingers through the widened crack to wrap them around the door's edge until her hand reflexively retracted from those painful vibrations again.

"Every time I try to push it, something *hurtful* pushes back."

Ms. Soffy thought about the door's hurtful surface, the seemingly deafening hum coming from outside, and the near-blinding light seeping in, and she came to these realizations:

"Bullies are in my way. They are pushing against the other side of this damn door. I'm talking about my past encounters with the bullies who're too busy believing in themselves to ever believe in *me*. *They* pushed me away and now, they keep me from my seat at the long table I dreamed of. They resented me because I was 'foreign' to them. The truth, justice, and common sense were missing from their judgments. The bullies' resentments were without merit and unfair!" She turned her back on the door to face the black void. "I've been taught that if you believe in yourself hard enough, you'll get what you want. But is that true? I just don't know anymore. It sometimes feels like everybody is trying *too* hard to believe in themselves. It's as if they're *hoarding* the power of belief and *all* of their attention is on vain pursuits, like how some people refused to spare any belief in *me*." She about faced to point a shaming finger at the door. "You bullies turned deaf ears and blind eyes to me. Rather than hear me out, y'all made your voices *louder* to drown out mine. Y'all made me less visible by making yourselves more *blinding!*"

She pictured his face in remembrance. He seemed to be the only stranger who believed in her at a time when she felt forsaken. He dared to not forsake her.

Harry Chinn promised to not give up on her and surely his promise would've been kept if he were still alive. She now drew strength from reflecting on how the baby boomer dared to not give up on someone who felt forsaken.

"I knew nobody in the big city. All I had was a little money saved up and my belief in myself." She addressed the harsh vibe radiating behind the door: "Going back to the farm was *my* choice. I don't blame the big city. No, it's my fault—I didn't get back up when all of your blinding and deafening ways pushed me down!"

Slipping her eight fingers through the slightly budged

open crack between the door and its frame and with both hands clutching, Hazel held fast and tightly to the edge—even though it felt like she was pushing on an electrified fence.

It hurt like hell and yet, she kept on pushing herself as hard as possible until finally, the crack widened by a few inches and the level of brightness and loudness went up a notch as the light and noise flooded in from outside.

She had pushed the door ajar enough to squeeze her arm through. With a thrusting jab, her entire right arm disappeared into the outside and as her upper body pressed up against the door, she felt the needling pain again, only this time in her shoulder, armpit, *and* chest.

She kept on pushing, refusing to give in and relent, determined to break through to the other side, summoning all the strength in her muscles and heart to do it, even though the pain could not be ignored.

Hazel *scream*ed like a blaring siren as her whole head squeezed through. She now faced the existence beyond the dark-triad prison.

While the door had her upper body pinned against its invisible frame, she looked outward to see a green meadow stretching far and wide under a blue sky. Only Hazel's head, neck, right shoulder, and arm had made it out—the rest of her was still stuck in the dark.

It felt like a thousand pins were pricking her nerves and the pain was more torturous than before. Miss Soffy could not take it anymore—the suffering was too much, and she fell into a state of surrender. She wanted to flop on the floor but, the squashing door had her body in a vice—keeping her pinned and upright instead.

She gazed dead ahead to notice what looked like a black dog running in the distance and this four-legged animal was cantering straight for her. The beast was a long legged one—completely matted in black, thick, and curly fur—coming at her in leaps and bounds.

In seconds, the gap between woman and animal was marginal and with a final leap, the beast pounced on her. She felt its hairy and strangely flattish face pressing harder and harder against hers as if it were trying to merge their eyes together!

The raven-haired animal was at least as tall as Hazel when standing on its hind legs. The black hair densely covering up its entire head made it quite indiscernible. For all she knew, it was a large and strange black dog trying to mash in her face with its.

Trying desperately to pry off the beast, she wedged her right hand in-between its face and hers—yet it never did growl nor bite her during the whole ordeal.

With one hand against its jaw, she managed to create a finger's width of space between their mouths as the "black dog" kept up the pressure on her face.

Ms. Soffy spat black hair from her mouth to plead, "Heavenly spirit, please come save me from the beast! Only divine intervention can tame the beast. My goal is to join the table and sit patiently with the other guests." The door's squeeze continued to cause stabbing pain along her upper body. "*Must*…get to…my group*!*"

THE UNFORESEEABLE

"You know...we can always forget about trying to save Harry too. Don't forget, calling it quits right now and not looking back *is* another viable option for us," the youngest Hazel suggested out of the blue.

They both said nothing back—her suggestion seemed to fall on deaf ears.

The trio had ninety minutes to go before the power channels through the tesseract for the last time. # 3 eased back on the reclining chair with a smug smirk on her face for she knew full well that the upper hand was hers.

She took comfort in knowing the latest clone to *pop* in from the future was indeed herself—which meant they're all on # 3's timeline now and everything would inevitably go according to her memories.

All I must do is act normal and let my destiny take its course. This is going to be a piece of cake, # 3 thought.

The outdoors lightened up as clouds parted. The cable ran from the 4-D machine's computer to the time-travel device on the original one's face. The phenomenal energy from the Beyond was going to cast the youngest Hazel back to last Friday—exactly half an hour before Harry died—hopefully.

The trio went over again how they could accomplish the mission by keeping enough nuggets alive inside the dome when the second cosmic blast comes—so that the youngest one could *pop* in on him and prevent his suicidal mistake with time to spare.

While they were finalizing their strategy, #1 cast suspicious eyes on # 3 yet again. As the trio practiced their duties inside the 4-D construct, #1 found it quite odd how little gusto # 3 was showing.

She squatted in the shaft, hugged their waists, and held them both up like a supportive brace as the duo pretended to fight off the toxic creepy crawlies in the dome, but all the while, # 3's eagerness to act as their pillar felt as phony as it did last light—she still wasn't showing them the gusto #1 expected from her. *Why do you seem so distant? How come your heart isn't in the mission? You'll only be letting YOURSELF down if you don't give the original one and me your all.*

Even though # 3 could sense her suspicions, it did not matter. # 3 did not care one bit if her attitude warranted disapproval.

She was too consumed by selfishness to be concerned with how others perceived her. Being the future queen of the Dark Triad was the only concern on her mind right now.

3 ultimately wanted nothing more than to serve only herself. There's a popular belief that, in order to be of better service, you must first help yourself. Yes, often our own needs firstly need attending to before we can possibly help others.

Dark triad followers, however, do not subscribe to that belief. Wasting your precious time and effort by "paying it forward" (as the saying goes) would only make you a foolish loser according to the Order of the Dark Triad because it preferred people who believed in ultimate selfishness.

The smug smirk on # 3's face was wiped off at 6:45 am. At which time, # 3 catapulted from the recliner and slid across the floor on her knees. Confusion started overwhelming # 3.

It wasn't # 3's conscious choice to scramble to her feet.

An inner force, rather, forced her to stand and dart glances at them both.

Meanwhile, # 3's five senses were in perfect working order, yet her mind somehow lost control over the body as if the heart had taken charge.

And then # 3 blurted out, "I'm not who you think I am! The Number Three you know is possessed by a Machiavellian-psycho narcissist. Standing before you WAS the other half of my split personality, but not anymore. I have escaped from Dark Triad prison to take back this body of mine! This is the *real* original one talking now." # 3 jerked herself around like a spastic freak at war with an inner demon. "Oh no…the dark triad personality is trying to come back and take over my body again. She *is* hurting *me!* Remember, Number Three cannot exist in the future if the mission gets accomplished, which is why she wants us to fail." She said to #1: "You shouldn't have been trusting me. Up until now, I've been wasting our time on purpose."

3 dropped to her knees when the funniest feeling came suddenly. # 3 felt a fluttering in her heart as if a soft-winged little bird were escaping from her chest. She felt it flutter out from her heart. Her head tilted back to look, yet there was nothing to see. Even though she knew it, whatever *it* was, had ascended skyward.

3's eyes shut tight, and she concentrated until her mind's eye could once again see inside the dark prison. What she saw with eyes shut was a thick beam of outside light flooding into the darkness.

The pitch-black door had apparently been opened wide enough for Hazel to have squeezed through it and # 3's mirror self—the better part of her—was nowhere in sight. The "true" Hazel had obviously escaped!

"Impossible, I couldn't have missed foreseeing what just happened. My future is all messed up now, now that I do not know what will happen next. How did she get away with altering events without me knowing?" # 3 then fathomed the mystery's reason and slapped her own forehead. "*Oh* yeah, I'm not the only one who owns the timeline we're on. My mirror-self came here from the future at the same time as me—she's as capable of skewing this timeline as I am."

"Number Three," #1 interjected. "You are a betrayer!"

Nobody needed the glasses to know what was coming next—#1 would soon be on # 3 like a dog catcher netting a cornered stray, but the charade was not completely over, yet. #1 took a step toward # 3 when the youngest Hazel crept up from behind and put the oldest one in a sleeper-hold to her surprise.

"Alright, the jig is up," # 3 admitted while seizing #1's flailing wrists as the youngest Hazel choked her from behind.

"We're *both* going to be the Dark Triad Queen, you see."

"Her death will no longer be like how we planned it. We have to kill her *now* instead."

"We can do it. It is two against one. Help me choke her out."

The youngest one squeezed her throat as tightly as she could and #1 verged on blacking out. She was struggling in vain to free herself from the clutches # 3 had on her wrists too. However, she still did have a choice: either succumb to losing consciousness or fight back hard.

Choosing the latter, she raised her knee up high to thrust one foot forward and kick the clone's midsection, *POW*—sending # 3 reeling backwards in pain.

She was still in the sleeper-hold, though. With both arms now free, #1 thrust one elbow into Hazel's gut and the blow caused her choke hold to loosen.

Using the strength in her legs, #1 thrust herself backwards and by doing so, she brutally rammed the original Hazel's back against the 4-D construct, *slam!* She had slammed against it real hard too, *zza-ap!*

Her back stuck to its side like magnetized metal on a magnet. The youngest one's body hair stood on end as amazing electric bolts flared from the tesseract, *zzt-zzt-zzzt!*

The emanating electric currents amassed into the shape of a giant hand. The newly formed "long fingers" stemming radiantly from the tesseract reached down and wrapped around the youngest one's body.

3 was still recovering from getting winded by the kick. She approached #1 who stood awestruck in front of the original Miss Soffy.

They both hesitantly watched on as the electrically radiant hand restrained her, *zzt-zzt-zzzt!* The youngest one pried herself a mere inch off the 4-D tool, only to be pulled right back up against it.

3 noticed #1 turn her head and she too looked away from their youngest self to see what the oldest one was looking at—and now they were both taking notice of the two time-travel devices left on the desk.

A surprise shocked them a second later when they looked back again at the pin-pricking tool, for their original self was no longer there—she had vanished into thin air in the blink of an eye!

#1 sprinted up to the desk and snatched up both time machines before # 3 could get her hands on them.

"Hand over those time machines to me," # 3 demanded.

"Never."

With a time-travel device in each hand, #1 bolted for the door without saying a word. The chase was on. While chasing #1 around the kitchen table, # 3 stopped by a knife holder and unsheathed its most lethal blade.

"There won't be any consequence for me if I kill you. I'd live on even after your death. Remember, you are a clone from *my* future," # 3 said with knife in-hand and the table between them.

"Go to hell."

She chased her a few more laps around the table until #1 put on the brakes by the fridge and when # 3 came running at her with the knife, *smack!* #1 had swung open the freezer door and # 3 ran face-first straight into it.

The next thing # 3 felt was a handful-sized slab of hard Parmesan cheese pelting her in the forehead.

"Ow," cried # 3. #1 grabbed another hunk of hardened cheese from the opened fridge and whipped it at her—the Kosher cheddar ricocheted off # 3's skull. "Hey, knock it off!" The cheddar was followed by a full brick of aged Gouda encapsulated in waxy rind, which squared her in the boob. "Quit it, *y*ou bitch!" A fast-flying pie of hard

Cojita cheese then struck # 3 in the buttocks. "OUCH."

3 ached from being bombarded by the cheese and while her back was turned, two hands grabbed the knife-wielding hand. With both hands clasped overtop of # 3's grip on the knife handle, #1 was like a monkey on her back who refused to let go.

#1 grappled her to the floor and she pinned # 3 after much effort. While straddling # 3, #1 pried the knife from her clutches and she plunged the blade into the Machiavellian-psycho narcissist's heart.

A stab like that would have killed *anybody* but, it did not kill # 3. Instead, the knife went intangibly in and out of her body as if she was a ghost.

#1 tried slashing her enemy's throat. The blade once again passed harmlessly *through* # 3 like a phantom object. Impossibly enough, # 3 cannot be killed by #1 no matter what! They stood facing each other.

"You can't murder me. I'm the younger you." # 3 cackled. "You couldn't exist if I'm dead. No paradoxes, remember? I am the cause; you are the effect. And no effect can exist without its cause."

#1 still had one of the time-travel devices on her. The other one had fallen on the floor by # 3's feet.

"The mission will be accomplished," #1 avowed when her mind's eye saw a flickering light.

#1 let the internal, pulsing light be her guide while dashing out the backdoor. She moved like a person without any time to waste. Regretfully leaving behind the other time machine, #1 ran fast into the woods like the speed of falling sand in an hourglass.

PRESCRIPTIONS

*M*s. Soffy found herself to be seated in an office cubicle with her head resting on the desk. How did she get here? She could remember her whole body being clutched by the giant hand with long fingers made of what seemed to be solid, yet benign, lightning.

Struggling against the radiant hand and the magnetizing effect the pin-pricking tool was having on her back as she stared back at the two Hazels standing a few feet away—those were her last memories before blacking out. Where did the cottage go?

The small cubicle had no decorative personal items. On the desk were a desktop computer, a swivelling lamplight, and a container containing standard stationary.

This did not seem like a dream. She felt wide awake. Hazel didn't know where she was. Was this the afterlife?

She swivelled around in the chair 180° to face another cubicle's back wall which was across from her on the other side of an eight-feet wide walkway.

Her head poked outside and looking left, she saw the identical cubicles lining both sides of the straight path. The two rows of uniform cubicles went on and on for as far as her eyes could tell and when Hazel looked to the right, she saw how the corridor ended at the top of a T-shaped intersection.

She climbed onto the desk to see over her cubicle walls. Hers was in a row of cubicles parallel to many more identical rows separated by their walkways. The rows and the walkways also crossed laterally to form grids. The sea of office cubicles uniformly stretched out endlessly in every direction across the flat expanse.

The high ceiling was as equally vast and florescent office lighting shone down on this land. When she swivelled around in the chair and faced the desk, the face of a gray sheep filled the computer screen as if right on cue.

"Your attention, please. Please identify yourself," said the onscreen sheep who, telling by her voice, was an ewe.

"My name is Hazel Soffy."

"Where were you sleeping before arriving here?"

"Where was I? I was wrongfully held captive in dark-triad jail."

They both stared at each other through their monitors in slack-jawed silence before the sheep sounded an alarm. *Whoop! Whoop! Whoop* whistled the strobe light coming solely from Hazel's cubicle. The siren went quiet to let their voices be heard as the warning light kept on flashing.

"Then...you're *not* the Hazel Soffy who was asleep at a cabin in the woods a few hours ago?"

"You're referring to my mirror self, the one with the dark-triad personality who metaphysically imprisoned me last light."

"Oh dear. I *knew* an error was made."

"Is it the other half of my split personality you're after?"

The ewe nodded *yes* just as another sheep walked in on the conversation.

"Hazel Soffy? My name is Arthur," said the ram standing in the cubicle's entranceway. "Looks like you flipped the wrong switch at the right time again, Candice."

"Are you accusing me of making a switcheroo mistake? Don't blame me, I was merely following instructions. It is my control panel's fault its buttons keep getting hit without being touched and the knobs wildly dial themselves. The uncontrollable glitches are worsening in the control room on the outer level, Arthur."

"Come on over then. Roam with me, Candice. Those of us who are on duty with the lions would be even happier if you were in here too."

"Where's your partner," Candice the ewe asked.

"Dewy is in the adjacent cubicle cranking the handle on the vice gripping some mean bitch's eyeballs."

"We must get this lady back to where she belongs."

"Although taking the best dosage is the correct option, I got a feeling prescribing her prescription will be my wildest adventure yet. Your reputation proceeds you, Miss Soffy. You are the beacon for your own most monstrous nightmare. Your demon has followed you here!"

"What? You *cannot* be referring to Dark Triad's mascot man-demon," Hazel said in disbelief.

"But he is, I'm sorry to say. I understand the man-demon was given two names in our realm: the Manmade Beast, and the Beast-made Machine," said the onscreen ewe.

"Yes, and it converges the path of savagery with the road to manmade artificiality while intent on merging humans into a fake reality. Dewy thinks it's drawing nearer.

He even tells me the time will come when it'll try to kill us. We three must get her prescription and fill it without delay."

"Understood. We'll be schooling for you back here at school."

"Roger. Over and out."

Dewy strolled up and stood towering over the talking ram when the video-chat screen closed.

"Where am I?"

"You are in-between schools, Hazel."

"Welcome to the land where bullies get taught by the bullied," Dewy said with an ear-to-ear grin.

Dewy was the most awesome lion she'd ever laid eyes on. His muscle-bound build was golden and more impressive in stature than your standard lion king as he must've been bigger than any big cat on record.

As his massive head leaned in closer to eyeball Hazel, something told her, *there is no need to be afraid* and so, she was cool like a welcome rainfall on a hot, dry day.

"You were brought to us by magic. Magic has everything to do with your reason for being here. Our alarm bells rang the moment you foresaw yourself poisoned by the Order of the Dark Triad last night. According to your case file: the magical way the ninety-year-old you possessed your body, the three tattoos you'll magically get tattooed on your back, and the rise of that darkly magic demon man—those things would be nonexistent if it weren't for the time-machine eyewear. There must be elements of magic in the tech. Magic must then go hand-in-hand with time travel," Arthur said.

"Your prescription is wedged under my chin. Reach in and take it but, be careful not to graze my skin, or you will feel severe pain."

"Humans always feel the sting of unworthiness whenever in contact with our flesh."

The lion let her dig into his bronzy mane, her fingers felt the hidden slip of folded paper, and she pulled it out. In her hand was a slip of 4" x 5 ½" paper and the typed info on it—the copy preprinted on the sheets of every doctor's prescription pad—was in a hieroglyphic language she'd never seen before.

Below the header of her legit note was the handwritten "drug info" which she read aloud: "Hazel Soffy…Thrill Pills…three doses…take as needed."

"Your prescription has got to be filled," said the sheep who stepped fully inside and sidestepped carefully around Hazel so as not to make physical contact with her. Arthur approached the desk's drawers and using his teeth, he pulled open the bottom drawer. "Drop it in."

The drawer was empty. "Will do." Hazel let the prescription slip fall from her hand to land on the bottom of the rolled-open drawer.

The ram nudged the drawer shut with his snout and then he ordered her to "look inside it *now*".

When she reopened the drawer, lo and behold, her drug prescription had vanished and in its place was a small, transparent pill bottle containing three light-green pills.

"What the heck do Thrill Pills do," she wondered.

"They nullify. Short-lasting yet potent, they're like hallucinogens," the lion responded. "Each dose can cancel out the automatic effect the path itself will inflict on you. Once you set foot outside your cubicle, the pathways' sensors will assume you're a convict of ours who is on the loose. At which time, our defense system's wrath would bombard you. The medicine will hopefully nullify the pain our built-in safety measures inflict as you make your way along the path."

"You'll also be needing somebody who's in a cubicle along the way to prescribe another drug."

Hazel stepped right up to where the cubicle's floor met

the carpeted corridor but, as much as she wanted to step over that line, the virtue of prudence kept her from setting foot on the walkway. She set her raised foot back down behind the line.

She twisted off the bottle's cap and let one pill slide down onto her palm before snapping the lid back on.

"You take one first. Here," she insisted while holding the pill close to Arthur's snout.

The sheep turned up his nose at her offering and looked the other way.

"Your prescription is meant for neither him nor me. We are free to roam our realm without taking any medication since it is us lions and sheep who OWN this entire security system," said the lion.

"We go undetected by your demon too. All of us talking beasts are too TRUE to be detected by it. We've made ourselves like ghosts to the Manmade Beast. The Beast-made Machine cannot take any offence at whom it is unable to see, hear, smell, nor touch."

"Dark Triad's mascot remains blind to the truth," Dewy said.

"Although, it will be able to see *you*, Hazel."

"The truth is like sunshine, and everything but the

truth is like the gloomy sky," remarked the lion. "Every man wishes to recognize the truth but, he won't see it because the mole rat has much in common with men. You see, the mole rat is as sensitive to 'sunlight' as people are to the truth. People cannot handle the truth! *The* truth is absolute. If the world did not filter and block the truth's light, the people who are like mole rats would go even blinder than they already are. People in the world depend on the untruth much like how mole rats need cloud cover in the daytime. So, you people keep on building more dark clouds to make your sky smoggier. You expand on the untrue to generate more untruths so that less light from above gets through to everybody. On Earth, everybody seems to be making it harder to get a glimpse of the truth for everyone else!" Dewy felt heavyhearted. "There's more to life than catering to the comforts of mole rats." He looked upward. "Thankfully, the truth sometimes does get through to the world when heaven drops *hints* on people. Hints like…when innocence is suddenly realized. Innocence is true, you see. Be it when a court of law does right by the innocent and rules in their favor. Or be it when a sweet little child expresses honest love. The truth is shining through the untrue in both of those cases. Or sometimes, instead of *answers*, the truth comes in the form of a question. You might wake up one morning with profound questions on your mind, such as, *how does heaven define me*? And you might also ask yourself, *what are my definitions of money?* Such soul-defining questions arise when a slight crack appears in a cloud of untruth to let a *ray* shine down on you. The light can pierce the clouds and for a fleeting moment, you get to feel warm from the sun, you see. And whenever a little truth seeps through the untrue, you get to *sense it!*" He *sigh*ed. "But people keep on contributing to the untruth. Rather than seek the truth and instead of following divine rules, people tend to fabricate and follow their *own* laws, for they want convenience and satisfaction too much. People want to enjoy the 'easy life' so much that they'll lie to themselves for it. They will focus on the more obvious gray in the sky rather than search for the enigmatic cracks in the clouds. And the untruth isn't just easier to follow, it's often the more pleasurable path too because the untrue fills one with a false sense of pride."

"You know what's more brutal than a false sense of pride? Living by the dark triad's rules, now that's brutal," the sheep bleated.

"Wait." Hazel did not forget. "The mission! Am I still able to complete it in time?" She chucked the pill into her mouth without thinking twice, *gulp*. "Which way, fellas?"

Scarcely had the lion bellowed "not so fast" when she hastily stepped out from her three-walled containment.

Alas, it was too late.

A hellish feeling enveloped her before she could step back inside. Every muscle in Hazel had seized up as the torment overwhelmed her. She had suffered similar feelings in the past. Only this time, the passion felt more devastating than ever before.

Hurt bombarded her like tidal waves against an old fishing boat in a bad storm. Hazel stumbled a few paces, toppled like a bowling pin, fell only a couple feet away from the nearest cubicle's entrance, and found herself barely able to move a single frozen muscle as if rigor mortis were setting in her body.

Her agonizing distress was a deep sense of longing. She felt a sense of loss as her "detachment" from everything "spiritual" was being realized! She was curled up on the walkway, hugging her knees, feeling physical pain, and missing dearly her spiritual connection.

It was as if the divine cord had been severed and no longer could she be honored by heaven's recognition. Nor was she able to get any respect from the heavens and no love from the elevated spirits either; nothing—leaving her with only one impulse: to die. Miss Soffy was presently having death wishes or in other words: a suicidal tendency.

"Ro-o-oll your body," Arthur drawled.

"Rock it too. Rock *and* roll, woman!"

The words "ROCK and ROLL", which they spoke in her ears with gusto, came not a moment too soon for she would've surely regretted idling on the pathway since a new affliction was sure to hit her at any second—and there was no telling what their system's automatic measures had in store next.

With the oomph to rock and roll herself, she rotated her stiff body a few feet along the floor and into the nearest cubicle. When she was confined by this cubicle's three walls, the anguish had remarkably left her as fast as it came.

The stunningly woolly ram and the massive lion came and saw her sprawled out beside a reclined dentist chair and strapped to it was a man with a high-tech apparatus over his entire head whose heavy breathing sounded like Darth Vader's.

Many questions were currently swirling around in her noodle but, before she could inquire about the oblivious man in this cubicle, the ram blurted, "*Baa-a-a-a-a-a-ah* yes hi, Hazel Soffy. How's bout yee? How in the name of Jaysus are ya? Alright there, Bud?"

"Your Irish accent is slipping out. Don't speak before your thoughts are fully formed, Arthur."

"You jumped the gun, Hazel. Give your medicine some

time to kick in."

When the steel sheet covering the man's private parts caught her attention, the machinery engulfing his face activated as though right on cue and caused an unseen force to rupture the thin metal with a *crack!* "OUCH," he cried as the splintered steel sheet fell from his groin to the floor.

At a loss for words, she stopped gawking at the squirming man to look back in awe at her new companions.

"You're witnessing a bully getting taught by the bullied. What we do around here is see to it that the bullied in your world get back some justice."

"We police," the ram added.

"Our interstellar machinery does a number on the bullies, turns the tables on their vices, and socks it to them with walloping virtues—while they're all fast asleep in their beds the whole time."

"Karma looks down at them and plots their demises while they sleep, Hazel. Your bullies are unworthy, wilfully ignorant, full of wrongful contempt, and they have the audacity to resent the respectable."

"According to our files, the man sitting here doesn't have faith in fascinating literature, won't benefit from reading any guidebook, and would laugh at you for receiving hope from a story book."

"This bully is in league with the 'bigger' bullies we've captured, which is to say, he desires a world where vice is king. Vanity, greed, lust, envy, gluttony, wrath, and sloth—those are the main vices he wants to live and die for."

"Acting conceited, stealing from the poor, being sexually perverted, contemptuously resenting others, habitually giving in to overindulgence, directing rage at the innocent, and laziness—we'll beat those seven behaviors out of him."

"How," she asked.

"By pummelling him with the very things his vices devalue: the virtues. As our automated devices confine him, he is getting slapped around by the hands of humility, generosity, chastity, kindness, liberality, patience, and diligence—the Seven Contrary Virtues."

"Our technology exacts revenge on millions of bullies in the world at any given time," Dewy chimed in with pride.

"Also, our machinery smacks them upside the head with the mighty Four Cardinal Virtues: prudence, justice, bravery, and temperance."

"We're working with the spiritual Three Theological Virtues too, don't forget: faith, hope, and charity."

"Follow your virtues. Do not let the vices lead you astray. If you let vice be a king, your world will get faker and phonier."

Hazel was abruptly distracted from their prattle and flinched when she felt an invisible hand scratch her throat. She jumped out in fright and into the walkway.

"Who touched me," she screamed at no one.

"The pill you took is working. Come with us," Dewy said.

The carpet under her feet crumbled, revealing an underground abyss, as she leapt toward the sheep who was following Dewy to the walkways' T-junction up ahead.

The floor kept on cracking wide open at her feet and up sprouted the natural earth as they strutted passed one cubicle after another—all the while she was able to ignore the painful airwaves the walls were transmitting.

The plant life behind her formed into an enormous arm which advanced by plowing its way through the flooring and she hopscotched further along the corridor to jump over its swiping, tree-like hand.

"Ow, it hurts," she cried out.

They both stopped and looked back to see Hazel down on all fours.

"Are you still having visions," Arthur asked.

She shook her head. "My visions are fading."

"Take another dose before it all fades away and the pills' effects might return instantly," said the lion.

She emptied the pill bottle's last two pills into her mouth without hesitating, *gulp…gulp.*

"Ye took two? Holy cow," the sheep exclaimed. "Massive thrills be coming to ye twice as fast like. Ye'll be sucking diesel and able to leg it in like no time!"

"Your Irish accent is thickening again," Dewy noted.

"Must be my Irish blood wishing to be heard. My ancestry comes from Shannon Ireland, ye know."

A hotly whitish humanoid face came out of nowhere as she struggled to pick herself up off the path. The smooth and hairless head protruded from a "rip" in the space six inches from her face.

The "being" she was face-to-face with appeared to be entering from another dimension. Its gender was utterly unclear.

The only thing she did feel sure about was its dislike for her. Its head floated closer and even though Hazel was still receiving the hurtful pangs, she shuffled away from the being as fast as possible.

She tried to keep up with the talking animals as the otherworldly being *and* the hungering plant life were hot on her tail. She turned right onto the intersecting walkway.

The ram and the lion were standing in the corridor a dozen cubicles away from Hazel and waiting for her to arrive. No sooner had she gotten close enough to smile at them both than the tip of *the* demon's stringy tongue latched around her ankle and tugged hard.

"Oh no, it's too late," Arthur screamed as they both saw it drag her by one leg down the path fast in the wrong direction.

THREE AGAINST ONE

She paced back and forth on the nearby forest trail behind the cottage while thinking about the three things which needed to be done within the next forty-five minutes. Firstly, she must get rid of # 3. Secondly, she needs to *somehow* bring back her original self and lastly, another clone must be reeled in from the future since the mission required *three* Hazels inside the tesseract when the killers come at 7:45 am.

Neither the time machine on #1's head nor the one which # 3 possessed could reel in any clones whatsoever seeing as how only the youngest Hazel had that ability. Chinn's eyewear made physical time travel possible for one's original self only—no more Hazels could *pop* in from the future unless the original Hazel came back from the sea of cubicles and used the glasses.

Hazel's clones from the future still had the option to foretell, though. #1 sped over the next sixty minutes to witness the mission's outcome at 8:02 am and this need-to-know moment showed her the sound and vision of dead air.

To be watching the fuzzy static could mean only one thing: #1 will have "bought the farm" by the time the cosmic power exists the 4-D tool. *Oh no... the timeline was altered. Now, my death will come even sooner!*

Several seconds into the premonition, #1 was even more taken aback when the hissing snow switched to an alternate reality where Hazel was alive inside the lab at 8:03 am. #1 was alternately foreseeing herself crawl out from under the pin-pricking tool but, a few seconds after that, the premonition of dead air appeared again.

#1 hit the 'rewind' switch. Time sped backward to 7:34 am—which was twenty-nine minutes ahead of the present moment—and she foresaw herself drowning in the lake. # 3 was pushing #1's head under water!

After a few seconds into the drowning, the perspective toggled back to the other reality where it was #1 who was dunking # 3's head under the shallows and at 7:33 am in this alternate timeline, the younger Hazel's face sprang from the lake only to receive the older one's knockout punch, *pow!*

The blow sent # 3 reeling backward with a *SPLASH* and then the perspective toggled to the other timeline where the roles of victim and victor were switched—she's now witnessing her own death by drowning once again: air bubbles rose from #1's face as # 3 pushed her head under the water, the oldest Hazel stopped breathing below the surface, and the severed telecast feed commenced at 7:35 am.

There's an explanation for this seesawing to-and-fro between destinies. If you watched the future simultaneously with somebody else, the timeline might split in two and if one more foreseer was added to the mix, then fate's single path could get divided three ways.

Time-travel glasses had the ability to create odds where there were none before. This ability to create probabilities explained how more than one destiny can exist when there are multiple foreseers influencing fate.

She calculated the odds by comparing the time duration of the snowy static to the intermittent 'clips' of the alternate reality. There's a 70 % chance #1 would lose the fight and die but, even though the odds were in # 3's favor, she still decided on being 100 % "sold" to her 30 % chance at staying alive.

There's always the temptation to "buy" stuff in the material world and so, people have always exchanged the things they had—such as money—for what they wanted. But perhaps money ought not to be ultimately for buying things. *Money ultimately ought to be for heaven! Money should be SOLD to heaven*, #1 thought.

"*But I am the money,*" alleged the little devil on #1's shoulder.

"*You're wrong! Everyone is the money,*" avowed the tiny angel on her other shoulder.

Something of yours, such as your cold cash, always got lost in the exchange whenever you bought stuff. We all eventually "*buy* the farm" too and the loss might be felt by others when we do.

Do not hate that feeling of loss, though. You can darken the heart by hating the loss you might feel after you "buy" something.

#1 *sold* herself to the minimal chance she had at punching out # 3 in the end. She was sold to the possibility like how baptizers sell babies to heaven.

She was NOT sold to it, mind you, like how a tempted and confused person might sell his sole to the devil. #1 was sold to her belief in herself like the word 'SOLD' slapped onto a realtor's sign on a house's front lawn.

Chinn's device allowed you to watch the future and witness the present at the same time. Like apparitions overlapping our reality, you could view your present surroundings and simultaneously see the future as a fully panoramic audiovisual hologram with a 360° tilt function.

They both were foretelling each other's next moves while being present to the here and now as soon as their brawl by the lake began at 7:20 am. They knew exactly what defensive and offensive measures to take since each of their hand-to-hand combat tactics were foreknown a second or two in advance.

#1 and # 3 reacted to each other's punches and kicks before they were even thrown because living in a constant state of foreknowing significantly enhanced their reaction times and abilities.

They applied bear hugs on each other while rolling down a hill. #1 and # 3 stopped tumbling near the dock by the lake where they scrambled to get back on their feet.

"You're insane. Only a crazy nut would attack oneself the way you are doing," #1 yelled.

"I'm being pre-emptive. You'll ruin me later if I don't finish you off now." They had to catch their breaths now. "Originally, our plan was to murder you at 11:35 AM. We would've strangled you after you throw up blood and collapse on the front porch later today."

"You mean to say that the youngest Hazel would've helped you suffocate me to death while I'm already passed out? So… the reason for my foreseen death is *not* because I ultimately sacrifice my health for the mission."

3 nodded and charged at her before #1 could ask *why*. It's too late to dodge # 3's running dropkick and #1 failed at Judo flipping her, *pow!* The blow knocked #1 down on her ass. # 3 dove onto her and they wrestled.

I wish I could freeze time, she thought while in # 3's headlock. #1 knew how the next seven minutes would be brimming with intense, nonstop action. #1 wished she could opt out of time's constant flow and come back to the present moment whenever she wanted. She did not want to go through the stress of having to struggle for survival. She wanted to be bored because boredom would have been a relief right now. She wished to feel antsy rather than be on pins and needles. She didn't want to account for every second until her time was up at 7:35 am when the static of snow either came or had not come. She did not want to worry about wasting time. #1 could take her sweet time to consider all the options before deciding on the "right" option, if only she could freeze time.

Their grappling match brought them onto the dock. They locked arms like two woodland creatures locking horns.

"We both know how you'll probably die in a few minutes," # 3 said. "Let me kill you sooner. The sooner the better."

"No, the *later* the better!" #1 put her in a choke hold. "I'm sold to victory!" # 3 elbowed her in the gut, squirmed free, applied a two-handed wrist lock on #1, and had her crying for mercy.

#1 soon wriggled out of the submission hold and she tackled her over the dock's edge, *splash!* They were both fulfilling their premonitions in the lake.

#1 had pre-set the watertight eyewear to keep on showing a few seconds ahead as she wanted to be her own echo. #1 hoped the slight delay would offer her enough time to come up with the winning moves.

3 had hers fixed on the moment #1 likely drowned to death. # 3 liked the odds being in her favor seven to three. Being the favorite to win made her feel smug.

Her eyewear had that final moment of #1's death by drowning on replay in a ten-second loop. # 3 was foreseeing #1's death every seven out of ten seconds and as they wrestled underwater, she enjoyed watching herself murder her.

They dragged each other down below the surface. #1 *knew* she was about to get kneed in the gut, but the blow could not be prevented considering how # 3 attacked from behind like an octopus on her back.

3's physical advantage was outweighing #1's foresight. #1 getting winded underwater was yet another piece of time's domino effect. She forced air bubbles from #1's lungs. #1 could sense the superiority #3 was feeling.

#1 swallowed a big *gulp* of lake water at 7:33 am. The slight chance of #1 living beyond 7:35 am remained slim and # 3's smugness haunted her. *Oh*, how she loathed the enemy for being smug.

DARK TRIAD'S MASCOT

The crimson-skinned, hairless demon man needn't any clothes and wore none, for it had no genitalia. It was agile, muscly, ripped, six-feet tall, and weighed in at two-hundred pounds. It ran inhumanly fast between the rows of cubicles—the sturdily-bridged nose on its weather-beaten face had picked up her scent.

This version of her demon was the most powerful one yet. Its big, black, sharp teeth and retractable, interlocking, finger-segment claws could easily shred through Earth's hardest metals. When it turned the corner and spotted Hazel, its tongue came streaming out as quick as lightning to grab her foot from fifty yards away.

"Oh no," Arthur screamed again.

Its tongue dragged her along the carpeted walkway like a lure on a fishing line being urgently reeled in. A second was all it took for the great lion to materialize and be seen leaping over her. Dewy landed between the man-demon and Hazel, stomping his massive paw on its tongue to keep it from dragging her any further.

He let out a super *ROAR* and the transparent wavelengths shooting from the lion's mouth were focused like a sonic-energy beam directed solely at the monster. His long roar blasted its body, sending it flying several yards backwards and *smash*ing through a cubicle wall.

"Blow it to smithereens," shouted the ram who came running over to Hazel.

Holding the snaky tongue still against the floor with his forefeet, Dewy bent down and bit it as hard as he could. Its tip let go of her leg immediately, flailed around in the air, and delivered a painful lash to his golden snout, *whh-tishh!*

The stunned lion stepped back, and the lengthy tongue fully retracted as fast as it had shot out. Dark Triad's mascot rose from the rubble before the dust settled and walked out of the wrecked cubicle to face him in a showdown.

"So, the jailer of my advocates finally reveals himself to me. Lion, I command you to release them all at once."

"I will when your home freezes over."

"Hell could be your home too, you know," it said with an evil laugh. "If only you would come around and see things my way, then you'd realize how intoxicating it feels to bully. Lion, *you* are the one who's THIEVING here, not me. You rob my advocates of the power I unleashed! I have taught bullies how to be great like the cold-blooded killer ant, and your reforms are taking that greatness away from them. Cold-blooded killer ants always get what they want, after all. That is because they are relentlessly merciless. They get away with wrongdoing too. A cold-blooded killer ant can even murder the innocent and not know guilt or consequence! The power of the cold-blooded killer ant is in them and yes, I unleash it. Bow down to the power of bullies! Bend to their whims or be devastated by them. Oh, what fun it is to watch the bullies benefit themselves when they sacrifice the lives of the innocent. I want the persistent bullies in the world to *always* get away with the crimes they commit on their way down to my home."

"I sure will love the feeling of bullying *you* to death between my jaws. It is time for justice!"

Its tongue unravelled super-fast at him, and the *crack* of a whip *snap*ped at his golden face as he got ready to pounce. The lion's leap covered the distance between them quickly, but the Beast-made Machine dodged his swiping front claws.

Meanwhile, the thrill pills' effect had worn off and Hazel was struggling on all fours to get sheltered by the next cubicle up ahead before the silent broadcast signals could make her pass out in the hallway from the pain.

"I won't let her beacon ever lose light" was Dewy's battle cry as the Manmade Beast grabbed him by the forelegs while its coiling tongue held off his ferocious jaws and yet, he managed to claw deeply into its skin. "BLEED, you no-good worthless bully. Don't you dare try to get by me!"

Dark Triad's mascot could cast a spell to teleport itself by using shadows as its means in this realm. The humanoid monster magically dove head-first into its own shadow in order to jump out of the one Dewy cast on the floor and instantly, it had flanked him.

It also took advantage of his four-legged disadvantage by using its humanoid stature to outmaneuver him. Its tongue held his ferocity at bay for the moment it needed to flip itself up and take him from behind.

Its ten torturous claws dug in deep, and it clung to him like a cruel rider on a rodeo bull. Dewy choked on the strangling tongue and try as he might, the lion couldn't revert to his ghost form while in its clutches.

It felt smug while riding and killing him up until his bronzy mane became radiant. The radiance in his chest grew into a silvery-golden aura. His glowing chest and forelegs transformed into a brawny humanoid upper body.

The encompassing glow made his hind legs more human too. He now stood relaxed at seven-feet tall. He reached behind himself and tore the six-foot tall humanoid off his back.

He overhead body-press lifted it to then drop its waist into his wide-open mouth, *crunch! Chomp*, its body came apart between the lion's teeth, *chomp!*

SPARKLER SPARKS

*M*iss Soffy crawled up to its entrance on all fours and no sooner had she fainted than a pair of hands reached down from inside the cubicle and dragged her fully off the path.

A few minutes later, light and dark fuzziness blurred her surroundings as she came to—at least the pain from the bombarding airwaves was gone. It took another minute for the eyes to discern the light from the darkness and she plainly saw an Irish man in his mid-forties kneeling over her.

"You made it, Hazel. Mike Kelly is my name and I'm at your service."

Michael helped her take a seat on the chair as they

shook hands. He wore blue-collar clothes and was handsome in an unassuming way by her standards.

"Here's your next prescription."

He handed her a slip of 4" x 5 ½" paper and its info typed in the hieroglyphic language was the exact same as the print on the last prescription she received. The only difference between the two prescriptions was in the "drug info"—there were no words written under *this* legit note's header, only a hand-drawn copy of her Dark Triad tattoo: the black triangle encompassed by Psycho the Scorpion, Vellian the Spider, and Narc the Snake!

"I wrote you the one for Thrill Pills." He handed her the new prescription. "Prescribe this prescription back to me."

"How?"

"Arthur will be back shortly with your doctor's pad for you to copy down on it what I drew."

"Can't you prescribe it to yourself?"

"No. The pharmacists won't fill self-prescribed orders."

"How'd you get here?"

"Well…I was shaping metal with a mallet on my rooftop yesterday afternoon. I'm a metallurgy artist living in San Francisco, you see. An electrical storm rolled in as I was forging a kingly sword. As I struck the iron while it was hot, a bolt of lightning hit me! I am the freak casualty of a lightning strike at my makeshift ironworks. Look..." He activated the desktop computer, and its screen displayed an aerial view of himself lying unconscious on his apartment building's rooftop. "See? My 'physical' self is actually back at my workshop as we speak."

"You need an ambulance. Nobody knows you're up there?"

He shook his head right when Arthur came in crying—he was all choked up and his bleats were heartfelt.

"Killing the damn thing nearly killed him. His body was covered in deep gashes, and he bled profusely. Dewy told me he was poisoned on the inside by its acidic saliva. It penetrated and violated him! I pray for his speedy recovery back at our school," Arthur wailed.

"The lion went back to school," she asked.

Mike noticed the confused look on her face and how the sad ram was too busy baaing tearfully to talk.

"The sheep and the lion are from a schoolhouse in another dimension. I learned a little about their 'school' in the hours I've been stuck behind this desk."

"He is the best of them all," bellowed the sniffling ram. "Everybody at school looks to him for authority. He always protected everyone from anyone who tried to take advantage of the kind and the generous."

"He saved my life back there," she told them with tears welling in her eyes.

"He didn't make anybody feel inferior. The lion even made us sheep feel like we each can be as great as him. Whenever it was his turn to speak in front of the class, he always showed respect and appreciation for the innocence embodied by his peers. The journey of self-discovery is an ongoing high jump event. And when it came to the self-discovery 'high jump', the lessons he taught raised the bar on NO ONE." He *sniffle*d. "His wounded body faded away right before my eyes as he disappeared from the walkway. *OHhh*, the agony poor Dewy must've been feeling." *Sniffle*. "I don't want the lion to suffer. I hope for one to be faster than the speed of pain. Fast like the gentle pinprick one barely feels when the right nurse gives the injection."

She knelt beside the weeping sheep with her hands clasped in prayer and Mike did likewise.

"Please let the lion be healed quickly by his teachers and peers," she prayed as Mike turned his bowed head to whisper in Arthur's ear.

"If I don't get my body to a hospital soon, then..."

"Then you both haven't much time. Hmm...which one

did Candice say it was in? Oh yeah."

Arthur pulled open a top filing cabinet, jumped up, and dipped his snout in the drawer to magically plunge head-first through it.

"It'll be stumbled upon in no time, don't worry," his voice echoed inside the magic cabinet.

"What is it like at their school?" she asked.

"It is an otherworldly academy where lions and sheep fill the classrooms to study one thing: human audiences. These students watch class presentations on people gathered in other classrooms, theaters, arenas, churches, and any place else we human spectators get together. They learn about mass appeal…and the reasons to fear the hubris of the masses."

"What else did the computer show you?"

"The lions need to eat the sheep or else they'll starve. Be that as it may, the sheep-to-lion population ratio maintains balance. You see, the sheep live and die of old age quicker than the lions do. Before they sacrifice themselves to the lions, the eldest ewes give birth and the older lambs become sheep by the time the lions must eat again. More lambs are born while the eldest sheep become mutton and for the most part, the ratio of the two species remains one-to-one." Mike's smile faded. "The harmonious beasts were living blessed lives before the day the human 'bullies' showed up in their schoolyard. They mysteriously came from nowhere and started killing the lions for sport. Those damn sadists murdered sheep for fun too. They had to do something about the invading humans and so, a container was developed. They contained the bullies in this sea of cubicles, erased their memories of every talking animal, and then sent them back to Earth. And the society of talking animals have been experimenting on the bullies in the world ever since."

"Dr. Soffy's prescription pad is in here somewhere. I can smell it."

Only Arthur's hind legs were showing as he rummaged noisily through the magically deep drawer with his fore legs and snout, *clink*, *clang*, *tink*.

"Did you learn anything about the prescriptions," she asked.

"Yes, the pharmaceuticals are concocted by spirits from beyond the grave. For instance, the pills I prescribed for you were created by a young woman's *ghost* in the year 2008 during the winter's end. Her ghost floated down into a chemistry lab located somewhere in this dimension. On the shelves surrounding the female ghost were flasks, test tubes, medicine droppers, cylinders, jars, and bottles. The liquids, powders, and gels in the glassware which she found most eye-catching became the ingredients in her improvised cocktail, aka Thrill Pills."

"What *are* the ingredients?"

"They all are variations of essentially the same thing: pride. You literally swallowed your pride by taking her spirit's pill. We swallow our pride to cope with the world, you see. The ghost engineered her medicine to convert hubris into the cure."

"Why did the female spirit make it?"

"She benefited from the process. It was a fun learning exercise for her to invent the pharmaceutical. Also, when *you* benefited from taking Thrill Pills, her spirit earned favor from heaven."

"Finally," Arthur said while pulling himself free from the filing cabinet to hand over the 4" x 5 ½" doctor's pad in his mouth. She noticed how the preprinted hieroglyphic copy on each piece of paper in hers differed from Mike's prescription pad.

"You can now redraw the picture I drew for your prescription."

She held the emblem for the Order of the Dark Triad on the paper in one hand and her own doctor's pad in the other. A moment of silence arose—she was hesitating.

"You drew the Dark Triad's flag. How can I prescribe the dark triad after the way it imprisoned me? I want nothing to do with the dark triad."

"Dewy instructed me to draw it for you. He wanted you to draw it for me too."

"Wait, I wonder." Wanting desperately to change the subject, she asked, "Do I even deserve help from the dead?"

"Maybe not," the sheep replied. "The dead may have doubts about you both. The ghosts who observe your world tend to think too many people lack discernment skills. The inability to discern raises doubt like a drawbridge drawn up over a fortress moat. They have reason to distrust the living when humans raise their doubts. The ghosts are probably vexed with you all because they are witnessing the innocence being lost and stripped from your world. I personally think there are too many teachers and leaders on Earth whose heads are up their arses. The students and followers are gaining nothing but phony knowledge with low morals from their lessons based on fibs," Arthur shook his head in dismay. "There are too many wankers. You've got the laudy daws walking around with their noses in the air, letting on like they're royalty. You have also got the Holy Joes who think they are morally better than everybody else, those sanctimonious dopes. A lot of gits out there too, brutal they are. Yep, there are many dense people in the world. The living can be as thick as a ditch. You earthlings keep on acting the maggot. The spirits want to scram when they see you do things all arse-ways. It makes them wonder, 'How're you all any use?' A countless number of them became ghosts when they committed their own versions of The Riverdance. Life's cruelty made them feel like they did not have a snowball's chance in hell at living happily—Hazel, you can earn the spirit-made pharmaceutical by making the spirits believe otherwise!"

"What the hell. I have to face it *sometime*," she uttered with pen in hand.

She drew on the top sheet of her prescription pad—drawing the black triangle, the snake, the spider, and the scorpion. She tore the paper from her pad and handed it to Mike.

They dropped their new prescriptions inside the desk's bottom drawer and the ram closed and reopened it. Lo and behold, their prescriptions had vanished and were replaced with a pair of twin matchboxes.

Mike picked up his long and thin matchbox to look at the symbol for the Order of the Dark Triad on the casing.

Hazel flipped hers over to read aloud the labelling: "Hazel Soffy…one sparkler…ignite as needed."

Each matchbox contained only one sparkler and a matchstick. They both lit the handheld sparklers and flaring, flying sparks tinged their arms.

The sparklers brightened as they shortened and a quarter-way into the light shows, Hazel and Mike felt tingles running throughout their bodies—they felt like sparklers who were radiating sparkles from the flesh!

The two dazzling orbs grew to engulf them in brilliance and when the sparklers fizzled to their halfway points, white light became all that the eyes could see—*sizzle, tingle, ting, ping, snap, crackle, pop!*

Like waking up from a dream, she reopened her eyes to find herself standing beside Mike on the eight-feet wide walkway and in front of many oinking pigs. The pigs cluttering the straight path behind them were too numerous to count, Arthur was nowhere in sight, the ceiling disappeared, and daylight shone from above.

They both were not feeling any pain and hardly noticed themselves being pushed forward by the marching pigs. He took her by the hand as they walked with the ushering pigs along the pathway while Swing Era jazz was heard above the squealing and the *oink-oink*s.

The gentle music came in clear over intercoms which their eyes could not find and the catchy 1940's tune—the big band orchestra was playing—had a lead singer.

She sang, "Pardon me, boy... is that the Chattanooga Choo Choo."

Several yards up ahead, colorful peacocks wearing opened parachutes were dropping in—one after the other. The leading pigs trotted faster and the first peacock to land landed on the pig in the lead, *poof!* That peacock and the pig it fell on had disappeared inside a puff of billowy mist.

"I think we're supposed to be there when a peacock lands on a pig," she said while leading him by the hand and picking up the pace.

"Tell me your phone number!"

She told him it before they both caught up with the next fastest pig to lead the herd and just as another parachuting peacock landed on the three of them, *poof! Sizzle, tingle, ting, ping, snap, crackle, and pop*—dazzling lights harmlessly blinded Mike and Hazel.

THE DEADLINE

*S**woosh, pop, zap, zing, POW!* The next thing Hazel knew, she was opening the tesseract's hatch from the inside. She crawled out from under the 4-D machine right as #1 came in sopping wet and ran to her.

"I punched Number Three's lights out, found some rope lying around, hog-tied her on the dock, and ran back hoping to find you."

At 7:43 am, the original Hazel searched for one more clone to bring in from the future—it was strange how the eyewear would not let her fast-forward beyond 8 am, though.

No, it was not the static of dead air that commenced at 8 am. The eyewear simply refused to foresee past 8 am—as if there was no future.

Pop! "Number Four" came from 8 am—one second before time "froze" to be exact. "# 4" was under sixteen minutes older than her original self. # 4, #1, and the youngest one entered the pin-pricking tool at 7:45 am right on the nose.

The new duo slapped the toxic web weavers in the dome while #1 squatted inside the shaft and hugged their lower bodies tightly. They were fighting for the lamb-like and the lionesque.

They fought back against the toxic antagonists. They fought their hardest right up until the glorious power blew in and made her feel like a human sparkler once more—*sizzle, tingle, ting, ping, snap, crackle, pop!*

Twas 10:40 pm and the Good Friday cosmic blast would arrive in roughly half an hour. Harry Chinn was left alone in his lab, and it startled him when the metal hatch underneath the pin-pricking tool fell to the floor, *clang!* The first thing the original Miss Soffy did when she crawled out from under the 4-D machine was look at the time.

"How did…Hazel?"

"Harry, is today Good Friday?"

"Yes."

Mission accomplished. "*Phew.*"

THE LOOP

She came from Easter Sunday to warn him on Good Friday. She told him and the other "original" Hazel how tonight's attempt at traversing history would be suicide.

"Thank you for saving my life."

"I'm stuck in a time loop," she told her younger self and Harry.

This was in fact the sixth time she stopped him from going through with the experiment on Good Friday. This was the sixth time she had vanished into thin air at 8 am on Easter Sunday to traverse history and reappear back inside the 4-D tool on the day before yesterday!

The time loop kept her from getting any older. Hazel

would always come back to 10:41 pm on Good Friday being the exact same age as when she departed from the day after tomorrow at 8 am.

Harry believed her time loop to be Grandfather Time's way of fixing the paradox. You see, destiny would be paradoxical if anybody were to alter the present by altering the past—fate, by definition, must always be unalterable.

To avoid the paradox, Hazel had to keep on reliving the Easter weekend of 2018 repeatedly. Getting sent back in time by the cosmic blast's second coming was Hazel's fate and so, her timeline had to keep on resetting.

Mike Kelly called her on the phone the night after Good Friday. Apparently—and solely in Mike's case—only mere minutes had passed from the time the lightning struck him to the moment he regained consciousness on his rooftop.

When the time loop brought her back for the second time, she took the next flight to San Francisco and visited him—before even getting his phone call—at the hospital where he was recovering from being struck by the bolt.

They had much to talk about while she sat at his bedside. They shared an interest in buying all kinds of insurance—insurers make sure that the earners in the world do receive the benefits they deserve, after all.

The topic of family values and what their families mean to them also came up. What they both had in common was a way of seeing it: small families, mid-size families, larger families, or orphanages—no matter how you slice it, every family member there is had been given the means to become "worthy".

"And the moral of the story is," she asked.

He shoulder-shrugged. "We ought to get schooled by the talking animal students as well as learn from the animals in the world too."

The return flight brought her back in time for the phenomenon's second coming. She was ushered inside the cottage by the other original Ms. Soffy who handed her a time-travel device.

The younger Hazel said: "we've been going through your notes on every calibration you remember Harry applying to his devices over the course of the last few times the time loop had brought you back. Your notes and me have been helping him feverishly re-tune his machines since you took off yesterday morning. We've been foreknowing and reprogramming nonstop. I've lost count of how many times we've precognized our upcoming results. After he made the last system change a few minutes ago, I foresaw you standing right here with us at 8:03 am! Yep, your looping problem sure looked solved to me."

"The world will know *two* original versions of Hazel Soffy after today," Harry said.

Her eyewear was linked with the computer connected to the tesseract. The platinum-swirl pattern on top of the 4-D tool swirled speedily when the cosmic blast came through.

The swirling, silvery luminescence formed into the shape of a "flying saucer" which hovered up and zoomed straight down upon the Hazel wearing the time machine, *swwoooosshh*.

Consumers will buy "Chinn's Fortune-telling Visors". His foreseeing devices will be mass-produced and sold on the free market. Harry and the two original Hazels will be celebrated in the limelight.

They will also, however, receive millions of complaints about the way the eyewear occasionally shows false prophecies. The consumers' number-one complaint will be: the fortune-telling visors show future events that never actually come to pass.

His visors for the public need to show *some* costumers untrue visions of the future, though. The destinies of *some* must be shown incorrectly in order to keep fate singular—only when those consumers choose to stray from or follow the precognition will they in fact *stay* on fate's single, solitary track.

Only one viewpoint will always foretell the truth. It's the view, from the Beyond, on other side of the pinhole.

EPILOGUE

Mr. Chinn hadn't ever invited anybody over to his rented cabin before, until now. When he led Ms. Soffy into his lab in the bedroom, her mind was immediately blown by the site of it.

Her jaw dropped and as her eyes bulged at the four-dimensional machine, the lingering silence between them tortured him. *Say something. Remind me why it is I trust you.*

"Your secret is safe with me," she promised. The silence was broken.

"The peephole is but a pinprick. We can look through it to see beyond the third dimension and into the Beyond."

Multicolored fiber-optic cords ran all around the inventor's pinpricking tool— thousands of them, shimmering and glistening. The cords along its top glinted softly like platinum.

The 4-D construct was roughly four feet tall. It had a

flat, square surface for a top. Harry put his finger on the fiber optics which covered its top's four sides. His fingertip ran along their length. This flat square *appeared* to be tilted. Starting at the square's lowest corner, he ran his finger *up* the tilt.

The path along the tabletop-like square, however, kept *on* inclining— not one side ramped downward. His fingertip, without lifting off from the path, went all the way around the square. It was logically impossible but, somehow, his finger slid right back onto the incline's starting point.

He then pushed through between two platinum cords. His inserted fingers gently spread the cords wider apart. Underneath these opened platinum lips was a gold button.

Pressing the button caused a *whizz*ing sound followed by a *whirl*. Then the construct's deck caved in slightly to form a peephole for the naked eye. He pressed his face against the concaved fiber-optic cords.

After looking through the eyehole for a minute, he lifted his head off the pinpricking tool to stare straight ahead at empty space. A dazed wonderment filled his wide-eyed expression. He blinked a few times, drew a deep breath, and turned to her. While staring blankly at her, it hit him— life! His eyes watered and lips quivered as he broke down in tears.

"Sorry, it makes my eyes water every time I look. I go through *withdrawal* each time I snap back to reality."

"What does it show you?"

"See for yourself?"

She gave in to curiosity and prudently lowered her face onto the 4-D tool's fibrous surface. Hazel saw through the eyehole:

Brilliantly shimmering particles filled her view at first, like golden grains dancing inside invisible waves within a bright white setting and then when her eyes blinked, she saw a closeup, wide-eyed face in front of black setting— Hazel's face!

She was feeling her mirror self's feelings while viewing her own face and it felt, for want of a better word, "cosmic". As Miss Soffy stared back at herself, it felt like being squished between the positive poles of supercharged magnets and as their forces held her up in the air, she was tickled everywhere but, not in an annoying way.

She felt herself solidifying into solid light while the cosmos shone upon her— brighter and brighter— from every angle, yet there was nothing about its light that seemed blinding.

Power is not a means to an end. Power IS an end.

"Say what?" she heard him ask loudly.

Hazel lifted her face from the peephole. Her eyes reopened and her guts felt queasy as she readjusted to the lab's environment.

"Did I say something," she asked.

"While you were looking through the peephole, you said: power comes from the ends."

"I really don't remember saying anything."

"We can receive messages from the Beyond, although they're hard to remember. It's like trying to recall a dream after you've awoken." Harry winked. "It takes practice."

"What *is* the Beyond?"

Professor Chinn did not know what the Beyond was or if it could even be fathomed, let alone explained. Harry *did* have his theory about it, although he had the darnedest time trying to explain *this* discovery...

Stare into the Beyond for long enough and your "answer" will come to you. One day, Harry empathized with his mirror self for longer than he had ever done before—thirty-three seconds. He watched on in amazement, wonder, and tremendous awe.

Harry reeled away from the peephole when he got "it" and afterwards, every time the man looked inside his 4-D tool, the answer always presented itself immediately as though his heart had become a sanctuary for the meaning of the Beyond.

An incredible urge to share his findings came over him and he wanted to inform others but, the question was: "how?". It's not enough to explain the meaning of the Beyond using only words as no human language could capture its true essence.

Mere words don't do the Beyond justice. At least, not the extent to which it deserved. It's like asking you to describe your soul.

At the 33-second mark, something happened inside him. Intense sensations, thoughts, and emotions were channelling into him. He was a vessel for his mirror self.

His mirror self was bearing witness in the meantime. Harry witnessed *the* most "resurrectifying" event in human history. Even though Dr. Chinn didn't watch the event with his own eyes and ears, he was still there. Impossible as it may be, Harry was present during the time of Christ.

What took place over a period of days was witnessed in mere seconds. Those days fused together. A moment of clarity flooded his senses as he witnessed The Sacrifice through the vivid empathy.

Jesus said, "I come to do thy Will, O God." Jesus made seven statements during His time on the cross:

"My God, my God, why have you forsaken me?" When He said, "I am thirsty", the guards gave Him vinegar. "Father, forgive them, for they do not know what they are doing." One of the criminals on the cross with Jesus believed in Him. So, Jesus assured that criminal by saying to him, "I tell you the truth, today you will be with me in paradise." The apostle John heard Him say to His mother, "Dear woman, here is your son!" This apostle understood what the ever-compassionate Son meant and from that moment on, John would care for Jesus' earthly mother. "Father, into Your hands I commit my spirit." The sins of the world were placed on Him. "It is accomplished!"

Then he mourned. Harry Chinn felt the loss. It felt like his body was being torn apart from the inside out. Never did he share the details of this hurt to anybody.

In the next instant, his mirror self healed and he was himself again. The inventor was ready to witness, through his mirror self, His Resurrection.

Once again, he can't see nor hear what's happening. Mr. Chinn was still merely experiencing the absorption of the experience. Living vicariously through his mirror-self allowed thoughts and feelings to be put *inside* Harry. Witnessing The Resurrection was experienced from within.

Mary Magdalene was the first to see the risen Son and announce His Resurrection publicly. As Mary wept outside His tomb, she at first mistook Jesus for a gardener. Then she realized the truth. She then wanted to reach out and hold onto Jesus.

"Touch me not; for I am not yet ascended to my Father," He told Mary, for what she needed was the faith to let go.

Also, for the sake of faith, the apostle Thomas, on the other hand, was granted permission to touch Him. Thomas, who refused to believe The Resurrection's eyewitnesses, stated, "(Until) I shall put my finger into the print of the nails, and thrust my hand into His side (where the spear wound was), I will not believe."

Jesus then said to Thomas, "Reach hither my finger, and behold my hands; and reach hither thy hand and thrust it into my side: and be not faithless but believing."

Thomas did so and said in awe, "my Lord and my God."

Jesus replied, "Thomas, because thou hast seen me, thou hast believed: blessed are they that have not seen, and yet have believed."

When the risen Son of God ate supper with His disciples, Harry Chinn was there too! The disciples didn't recognize Jesus at first but, when they finally did, He disappeared before their eyes. It was as Luke says: "Their eyes were opened, and they knew Him; and He vanished out of their sight."

Empathy came, via Chinn's mirror self, for those last moments on the mountain in Galilee where He had assembled the eleven apostles. Jesus said to them, "…teach all nations…in the name of the Father, and of the Son, and of the Holy Ghost." Before He took off into heaven, His last words were: "I am with you always, even unto the end of the world."

Every event has a place in time's fabric. The time-machine charger pricked the fabric of *that* time.

It's The Sacrifice and The Resurrection. Witnesses were devastated and then uplifted. Those few days were experienced as one sudden, empathetic moment for Harry.

"The Beyond is the embodiment of His Sacrifice and Resurrection. Access to the Beyond is a gift from the Holy Ghost. Those are my beliefs."

"Are you taking power away from the Holy Spirit?"

"No, Hazel. The power is given generously*!* The Holy Ghost compelled me to make the peephole."

Plugged into the pin-pricking tool were both pairs of time-machine glasses.

"What do those techno eyeglasses do," she asked.

"They serve the future."

Printed by Libri Plureos GmbH in Hamburg, Germany